THE BIG MAN'S
DAUGHTER

Inquiries should be addressed to
Start Science Fiction
221 River Street
9th Floor
Hoboken, New Jersey 07030
Phone: 212-431-5455
www.seventhstreetbooks.com

10 9 8 7 6 5 4 3 2 1

ISBN 978-1-64506-019-2 (paperback)

ISBN 978-1-64506-020-8 (ebook)

Printed in the United States of America

THE BIG MAN'S DAUGHTER

a novel

Owen Fitzstephen

SEVENTH
STREET
BOOKS®

"All of my characters are real. They are based directly on people I knew, or came across."

—Dashiell Hammett
New York Evening Journal, 1934

Huston waved his big hands in the air. "Frankly, Dash, I can't help wondering why she's in the book at all. I mean, she's only got that one scene with Spade in the Fat Man's suite. And when the book's over she's the only character unaccounted for . . ."

"Look, it's been a long time since I wrote that book," Hammett acknowledged. "Hell if I remember what I was thinking when I put the girl in."

Huston nodded. "So, what happened to her after all the shooting was over? The real girl, I mean. The Gaspereaux girl."

—John Huston and
Dashiell Hammett in conversation

From *Hammett Unwritten,*
a novel by Owen Fitzstephen

CHAPTER ONE

The smallish girl of eighteen, Rita Gaspereaux, placed her right hand into the consoling hands of Theodore Blaisedale, the funeral director who had asked her to join him for a moment alone in his office. Even here, even now, she could not help noting that his cutaway morning coat and striped trousers seemed better suited to the Belle Epoch—her father's generation—than to these days, the Twenties, when simpler, more business-like attire best expressed the "serious" professional man. Rita considered what wearing such old-fashioned clothes suggested of a man not more than thirty years old. Had Blaisedale an overwrought sense of the romantic past? Or a taste for formality that ran to religiosity? In either case, he would be an easy mark for a pretty girl of eighteen who was well practiced at confidence games. For such a man she would play the damsel-in-distress, Rita thought. She had done it a hundred times before. Life with her father had taught her to consider all human characteristics as vulnerabilities. The way a man walked, the way he sat, the way he spoke, the way he dressed—one need only observe, analyze, and then create a fiction suited to the circumstance. She closed her eyes as if falling into a swoon, and leaned into Blaisedale, who could do nothing but hold her up.

"Miss, are you all right? Miss!"

In the past, she'd have continued the ruse until she seemed to lose consciousness. A dead faint provided opportunities. Matrons, who only a moment before might have felt jealous of the girl's beauty or youth, would flutter about her suddenly unconscious form, regretful for their resentments, sentimentally identifying her vulnerability with their own lost girlhoods. "Let the poor dear breathe!" they would cluck. And any man into whose arms Rita fell (whoever he might be) would discover within his embrace the meager weight of her body, the porcelain smoothness of her face, the softness of her hair against his neck, the sweetness of her breath, before discovering in his own "heroic" heart a sudden, almost overwhelming sense of responsibility for her welfare, whereupon Rita would "regain consciousness" to a world more amenable to her desires than the one from which she had departed just a moment before. She had been taking advantage of such maneuvers since she was six years old. But now, after initiating the ruse in the funeral director's office, she stopped herself short. She was not here, after all, for business. At least, not the sort of business to which she was accustomed.

This visit was legitimate.

She straightened in Blaisedale's arms, stepping away from him.

"Are you all right, Miss?" he repeated.

"Yes, thank you." She had no intention of scamming the undertaker. She was through with all that. "We can just get on with things. You said you wanted to talk to me?"

"Yes, your late father . . ." Blaisedale said. "The shock of the circumstances . . ." He shook his head. "It's unimaginable."

"I don't know if I'd go quite that far," she answered, sitting in the plush chair he offered her beside his giant, uncluttered desk. "The imagination can be a powerful thing."

"You may feel alone now in the world, but you are not," he continued.

Yes I am, she thought. Even her father's business associates were gone. Of course, none of them had ever been trustworthy or reliable. Nor had they ever shown much interest in Rita, except as a vehicle for their schemes. Nonetheless, she couldn't help missing them a little. Emil Madrid, for example—for all his preening, lilac-scented, self-centeredness—had taken her to the opera a few times, translating the Italian for her at critical plot moments. And once in Greece he had introduced her to his aged mother as his "little American Aphrodite."

Likewise, red-haired Moira O'Shea, the most beautiful "older" woman (over twenty-five) that Rita had ever met, had taken time these past months to instruct her on finer points of make-up and hairdressing that were not to be found in the advice columns of the fashion monthlies. Wilbur Clark, her father's bodyguard and murderer—a nasty little bastard—had once put a jazz recording on the gramophone in a hotel room in New York and taught Rita to dance the Charleston. She hadn't even minded when he kissed her that night—that is, until he became drunk and slobbery. And Floyd Bradley had taught her to smoke a hookah in Casablanca and to roll a marijuana cigarette in Juárez, though she could not claim to have ever enjoyed his company. Still, so many of them dead. And the others in prison.

Yes, she was alone. "You said you had some 'special concerns' you wanted to discuss with me?" she asked.

Blaisedale focused his eyes upon her with the same practiced expression of sympathy she had seen before in the eyes of countless funeral directors. Of course, most people do not know that what is said and done in such places as this is so standardized. Most people only bury their father once. Still, she thought it strange that this occasion should be so little different from the many other times she had been comforted for the loss of a father by one or another embalmer as saccharine as Blaisedale.

Well, authenticity was bad for her business too, she thought.

The funeral swindle worked like this: Rita's father Cletus Gaspereaux (known to some in the rackets as the Big Man) would visit a morgue in whatever city he and his daughter were currently residing. There, he would claim to be looking for a brother who had gone missing a week before. Medical examiners would show Gaspereaux whatever unclaimed "John Doe" bodies had recently been discovered in back alleys or floating bloated on the river or stinking up a flophouse bedroom, at which time Gaspereaux would identify one of the corpses as that of his brother and proceed to make arrangements for its delivery to a mortuary under the care of this fictitious brother's fictitious "daughter," for whom he naturally gave a fictitious name. The city morgues were always happy to clear space. A few days later, Rita would arrive at the mortuary in the role of the grieving daughter from out of town. For these occasions she wore her black dress and her pearls, cutting a lovely and prosperous figure. Same as she wore now. Tears, grief, a dead faint . . . always the same. At last, after arranging a funeral fit for an emperor—complete with a hired string quartet, local soprano, ebony casket, artisan-fired death mask, leather-bound memorial booklet, cemetery plot with a view and four foot granite headstone with sculpted angel—she would remove her alligator skin checkbook to pay to the by-now charmed funeral director a fee of two thousand dollars or more. At the last moment, however, she would ask him to advance her a few hundred dollars cash ("Which I'll be most happy to write into the total of my check . . .") so that she could immediately wire funds to relatives for rail passage to the funeral. Otherwise, as local banks might not cash her out-of-town check, the whole funeral would have to be postponed. Just two or three hundred dollars . . . What could the funeral director say? Didn't he already have repayment of the cash written into the bank check he held now in his hand? And didn't he possess the father's body as collateral for the check? Besides, how can you say no to a grieving girl, especially a pretty one? "Maybe you could make it four hundred," Rita would add. Naturally, the out of town bank check was no good.

The undertakers' cash was always good.

What became of the bodies was anybody's guess.

Some large cities had as many as five or six morgues and up to two dozen funeral directors, most of whom were reluctant to admit to their colleagues (or to the police) that they were ever swindled. Such admissions are bad for a funeral business, which presumes to be the most dignified business of all. The Gaspereauxs could take up to a thousand dollars from funeral swindles in any one city.

But today was different.

This time, the corpse in the next room actually belonged to her father, which may have been why Rita was finding it more difficult now to act grieved than on any of the previous occasions, when she at least had felt no animosity for the anonymous corpses laid out on slabs, her false fathers.

"Your father was a man of diverse interests, I assume." Blaisedale moved around to the other side of the desk and sat.

"You could say that."

"Your father's place of birth?" Blaisedale asked.

Rita was not sure if anything she knew of her father's past was true. He claimed to have been the only child of a wealthy merchant family in Bern. "Switzerland," she said.

"Ah, he traveled far in his lifetime."

That, at lease, was true.

"Tell me about your father," Blaisedale asked.

Gaspereaux had been educated in English boarding schools; when his family lost their fortune in reckless speculation, he left school for London where for a short time he wrote a column for a Fleet Street gossip page before joining a crowd of underworld types whose diverse and profitable business enterprises spanned the breadth of London. Among them, Gaspereaux thrived, his inventive mind useful not only in East End alleys, but also in the private boxes at Ascot, where horse races proved little more difficult to fix than dice games down on the Thames. Soon, he was no longer taking orders but giving them. "I eventually sat like a spider at the center of a great web of criminal enterprises," he bragged to Rita. However, a consulting detective of some repute ("You'd recognize his name, my dear . . .") eventually drove Gaspereaux from London; he fled to New York City with a trunk-full of cash and appetites large enough to consume the world. There, he drank only Johnnie Walker and smoked only Coronas del Ritz. This impressed young Polly Shaw, a chorus girl whose tastes in men had more to do with diamonds and promises than physical attractiveness. Gaspereaux was her guy and their three-week affair made up in passion for what it lacked in longevity. When he left New York City for Paris and other promising continental locales he did not know that Polly Shaw was with child and did not learn he was a father until almost six years later, whereupon he traveled to an orphanage in New Jersey to take young Rita as his charge. Or at least that's how the story went.

The orphanage part was real, as it was the first home Rita remembered.

After Gaspereaux claimed his five-year-old daughter, the two lived together in a strange, cosmopolitan whirl. One city after another . . . Driven not only by immediate exigencies (such as occasional "mix-ups" with local police or mob bosses), but also by Cletus Gaspereaux's relentless pursuit of a statuette he called the Black Falcon, about which he explained nothing to Rita, claiming that ignorance was her best defense against the evils of the world. Now, she hoped that as he lay dying the last thing he felt was regret for having failed to acquire the bird. But dying was probably distraction enough to spare him, which is why she hoped there was an afterlife—so he might be regretful now. "I don't see how my father's history relates to our business, Mr. Blaisedale."

"He was a bit of an adventurer?" Blaisedale pressed.

"Well, he died an adventurer's death."

"Do you have a mother, Miss Gaspereaux?"

"She did not survive my birth."

"Then you're on your own?"

"Oh, I have many friends," she lied. "They're anxiously awaiting my return home."

"And where exactly is home?"

She had always lived hotel to hotel. "New York City," she said.

"And what are your plans for the future?"

Her plan was to begin using some of the mail-order beauty products her father always insisted were no better than snake oil—like "Ingram's Milkweed Cream." Finally—and most importantly—she would catch a southbound train to Hollywood, where she planned to become a motion picture actress. There, she would adopt a new name: Celeste Star, Camille Bloom, or Lilliana Raintree—all better names than Rita Gaspereaux, which she thought sounded like a painful stomach ailment. Mr. DeMille or Mr. Griffiths or Mr. von Stroheim would doubtless help her decide which of the prospective names best fit her soon-to-be-discovered persona. But she told Blaisedale none of this. She had learned from her father that information, like everything else, was a commodity to be purposefully spent, never squandered. And more—he had taught her that "the fish that opens its mouth once too often is the fish that gets caught."

"What field of endeavor will you undertake?" he pressed.

"'Undertake'?" she said, smiling. "That's a fine word for an undertaker to use."

"We prefer being called 'funeral directors.'"

"Of course, I'm sorry."

"You're not planning to follow in your father's footsteps, are you?" he asked. "Professionally speaking, I mean."

"That's an impertinent suggestion, Mr. Blaisedale."

"Merely direct."

This was not ordinary funeral director patter. "If you must know, I'm going to Hollywood to become a motion picture actress."

He laughed. "That's a good one."

"What's that supposed to mean, Mr. Blaisedale?"

"Another of your fictions?" he asked.

"What, fictions?" She wondered why he was not delivering the standard God-loves-you and you-are-not-alone hokum. And who the hell was he to doubt her future in Hollywood, anyway? "For your information, Mr. Blaisedale, I'm quite well suited to becoming a film actress," she said. This she knew because she had written a few months before to the Film Information Bureau of Jackson, Michigan, for their *Twelve-Hour Talent Tester* and *Key to Movie Acting Aptitude*. Results indicated she was more of a Constance Talmadge than a Mary Pickford. (Yes, she was petite like Mary, but her dark hair and eyes gave her an air of mystery that "America's Sweetheart" lacked.) She had been unable to complete the correspondence course because she lacked a permanent mailing address. But with as high a natural aptitude for movie acting as the test indicated she possessed, she believed she hardly needed schooling.

"One of my favorite actors is Lon Chaney," he said.

A horror star—it figures, she thought.

"I have gained many professional insights from observing Mr. Chaney's movies," he continued. "Of course, I'm no actor myself. But it's not his acting that provides me with professional insight. It's his expert use of make-up."

She had seen *The Hunchback of Notre Dame* the previous week—just before all the killing started.

"He takes a perfectly ordinary face, his own, and turns it into something quite grotesque," he continued. "Whereas in my profession, I am sometimes required to take a grotesque face, damaged in an accident or a shooting or any number of mortal misfortunes, and make it appear ordinary. For open casket viewings, of course. That is why I am a student of make-up and prosthetics. Do you see? I'm a Lon Chaney in reverse."

What was he going on about? she wondered.

"Your father's face would pose just such a challenge," he continued. "If we'd done an open viewing, that is."

Rita stood, outraged. "Look, I didn't come here to be mortified by the details of my father's death."

"What did you come here for, Miss Gaspereaux?"

"Comfort, of course. Consolation."

"That's not what you came for last time," he said.

"Last time?"

"Eighteen months ago," he explained. "Your father had died then too. A different father, of course. I believe I made you a loan, by which your relatives were to travel here from Michigan."

Her breath caught in her lungs.

"I believe you wore the same dress you're wearing now," he continued. "Yes, and you wrote me a check, which the bank failed to honor. But by then you had disappeared."

It was possible. She and her father had passed through San Francisco about that time.

"You can imagine my surprise when I saw you here today," Blaisedale continued. "Along with the body of your real father."

She said nothing, but gathered herself.

"That is," he continued, "if he is your real father."

How was one to distinguish between one undertaker and another when they were all so much the same? Damn. This was her father's fault. Cletus Gaspereaux had never made notes (again, for fear of incrimination) but kept the history of their business dealings in his head.

"Is he?" Blaisedale pressed.

"Is he what?"

"Is he your real father?"

"Of course."

"That's what I assumed," he said. "You paid in cash this time."

This would require delicacy.

"I know who you are and I know about your business," he said.

She considered how to play him. "Everybody knows, now. My family's tragedy is in all the newspapers."

"Tell me about this 'Falcon.'"

"My father never talked to me about it."

He looked at her with disbelief.

She quoted from memory what she had read the day before in the newspaper. "The Falcon is an ancient statuette whose creation remains shrouded in mystery. The *objet d'art* entered western lore in the fourteenth century when the Knights Templar offered it as tribute to a French king. While it appears to be only a slightly interesting *objet d'art*, rumors that it possesses 'mystical powers' make it worth a king's ransom . . ."

He stopped her. "I already know that."

"I'm sorry. I only know what the papers say," she answered.

"What 'mystical powers'?" he pressed.

"Neither my father nor any of his associates ever trusted me with that information."

"That's hard to believe."

"It's true." And it was. As a girl of seven or eight, overhearing adult conversations about the Falcon's presumed whereabouts, she had imagined it to be a spectacular, living bird (though she found no mention of such a bird in the ornithological books she slipped past naïve librarians who recognized "theft" only as a word that appears in the dictionary between "thee" and "their.") By listening at keyholes, she eventually discerned that the Falcon was an object about the size of an American football, and that it was worth a fortune. She knew nothing more, except that the thing served as the object of worship in the pagan life her father fashioned. And so she always disdained it.

"Your late father and his associates mistook a counterfeit for the real thing?" Blaisedale pressed.

She nodded.

"But why did your father's bodyguard shoot him?"

She looked away. "My father was planning to give Wilbur up to the police as a fall guy."

"For the murders?"

"Yes."

"And your part in all this?"

"Why do you care?"

He shrugged. "I'm a concerned citizen."

A morbidly curious, goose-necking son of a bitch was more like it, she thought. But she withheld her anger. "I had nothing to do with any of it."

He said nothing.

"That's why the police let me go," she continued—though, in truth, it had likely been the sympathetic note to the department from the private detective who had broken the case that had done the trick for her.

"Well," the undertaker said, his expression growing arrogant, "I rather suspect that with one little word from me about what transpired between us last year in this office, the police will be delighted to put you right away, whatever their previous attitude."

"Yes, that's possible," she answered, calmly. This was not the tightest spot she had ever been in. There had been a gendarme in Paris who once clapped her into handcuffs, and a sheriff in San Antonio who once locked her up for a whole night. She considered the undertaker—he seemed manageable. Her father had not taught her all he knew—but he had taught her a lot. She smiled at the undertaker. "The truth is, Mr. Blaisedale, I'm quite relieved."

"Relieved?"

"I was afraid you'd forgotten me."

"What?"

She looked away, suddenly shy. "You're not going to make me spell it out for you, are you?"

"Spell what out?"

"When it seemed all this time that you'd forgotten me . . . well, I was cut to the quick."

"Look, what are you talking about?"

"Wait." She reached across the desk and touched his hand. "You're not . . . No, that's impossible. You can't have thought my returning here was some sort of accident, can you?"

"Why else would you return to the scene of the crime, Miss Gaspereaux?"

Scene of the crime . . . She suspected he'd read one too many issues of *Black Mask* magazine. Good. She could make that work for her. "I've returned because of you, Mr. Blaisedale."

"Me?"

"We shared a spark last year in this office," she said. "Please say you remember."

He said nothing.

"You were so humane and sympathetic," she continued. "You've no idea how many times this past year I've recalled the way you took me in your arms, comforting me when I broke down in tears."

"It's part of my job," he said. "At the time, I believed your father had died."

"Now he has."

"Yes, and what of it?" he snapped. "You seem to have forgotten the nature of our last encounter."

"What matters is how I felt when I was in your arms."

"What?"

"Was I wrong?" she asked.

"About what?"

"About how generous and understanding a man you are."

"You cheated me, Miss Gaspereaux."

She sighed. "I'm not a bad person. Please believe me. All my life I've been a mere hostage to my father's criminal activities. How could I resist him, Mr. Blaisedale? He was a bona-fide, criminal mastermind." She knew he'd like that term. "You've read it yourself in the newspaper."

"But why would . . ."

She did not let him finish. "I've come here," she interrupted, "to ask forgiveness for the crime my father and I committed last year against your generosity and goodwill."

He was taken aback. "So you returned on purpose?"

"Yes, of course."

"Then why have you said nothing about 'forgiveness' until now?"

"I told you." She looked away again. "I was afraid you hadn't recognized me."

He said nothing.

"I know I'm not the most 'memorable' looking girl in the world," she continued, aware that the contrary was closer to the truth.

"Oh, that's poppycock!"

"Then you do like the way I look?"

"I mean your whole story," he answered. "You expect me to believe I was the only businessman you and your father cheated, Miss Gaspereaux?"

"No," she said. "There were many."

"And you're planning to ask all of them to forgive you?"

"Don't you understand? I've come only to you."

"Me? Why?"

"Because you're different, Mr. Blaisedale." She leaned across the desk. "You're a man of integrity and kindness."

"You're not being sincere, Miss Gaspereaux."

She looked surprised.

"Do you take me for a fool?" he pressed.

"Heavens, no." This was going to require more than mere flattery, she realized. Now was the time to turn up the heat. "You're such a successful man," she said. "Why, just look around this office. Isn't that an award from the Chamber of Commerce?"

He nodded. "Most women are put off by this kind of work."

She noticed he wore a gold wedding band. That was good. She recalled her father's description of the fish that opens its mouth once too often; accordingly, she cast a new line, hoping he would rise. "I happen to find the work you do here to be erotic. Perhaps that makes me unusual. But here we are and there's no sense denying it."

He said nothing.

Ordinarily, she would now invite him back to her hotel suite where she would give him a drink, flirt, and then remove his clothes before taking him onto the bed with her; after a few slobbery minutes, she would call his name loud enough to be heard in the next room, whereupon her waiting father would burst onto the illicit scene, outraged that his "innocent" underage daughter was being ravaged. Sometimes

Gaspereaux entered with a pistol; sometimes he merely picked up the telephone and threatened to call the hotel detective. Blaisedale (or whoever) might claim innocence, but his nakedness would undermine his defense and force him to propose a "settlement," which Gaspereaux would refuse on principle a few times before finally agreeing to accommodation. In the end, Blaisedale would make it out of the suite only by leaving behind a gold pocket watch or a diamond pin or the contents of his wallet (in addition to forgiving last year's debt). Blaisedale was a perfect mark—naïve, respectable, and as corrupt as the next guy. But Gaspereaux would not be in the next room anymore to enter brandishing his pistol, outraged and dangerous. Rita was alone. But she was not yet beaten. "I'm not displeased that we're here together, Mr. Blaisedale."

"You're not?"

She shook her head no, allowing him to sort through his options. She knew where they would take him, sooner or later. He was a man, wasn't he?

"Well, what can we do about this situation?" he asked.

"I have no money," she said.

"Then how are we to find an accommodation?"

"You do like me, don't you?" she asked.

He said nothing, but his eyes answered yes.

She nodded, encouragingly.

He reached out and took her right hand in his. Then, reflexively, he pulled away, having noticed that the hand was missing half of the pinkie finger.

She lowered her eyes. "You find my disfigurement offensive?"

He recovered himself, taking the hand back into his own. "Oh no, no." He stroked the half finger as if suddenly fascinated. "It just caught me by surprise. You poor thing. How did you lose it?"

The truth was she didn't know. No one ever told her details. So she shared with the undertaker all she knew. "Some sort of accident when I was an infant. Naturally, I have no memory of it. Probably just as well."

"I find it beautiful," he said.

No surprise coming from an undertaker, she thought. "Thank you, you're kind."

He raised her right hand to his lips and kissed the shorn finger.

She pulled the hand back. "Have you ever gone away for a romantic adventure, Mr. Blaisedale?"

He paused. "Of course."

His honeymoon, no doubt. "May I ask a favor of you?"

"Go ahead."

"Will you describe to me where you'd take me if we were to have a romantic adventure together?"

He looked confused.

"It'd help to set a mood, Mr. Blaisedale. I need a mood. And then . . ."

He attempted to disguise a smile. "Call me Theodore."

"Where would you take me, Theodore?"

"A hotel, I guess."

"Describe it to me."

He leaned forward in his large, leather desk chair. "And after I describe where I'd take you?"

"Well, when I begin to picture in my mind some lovely place that is *not* a mortuary . . ." She stopped.

"Yes?" he pressed.

"Then I'll come to you and you'll keep talking and then I'll put my hands on your shoulders and then I'll put my lips on yours . . ." Her breathing quickened just perceptibly. "And we'll go to the lovely place you're describing, without leaving this room."

"Where I'm sitting now?"

"Yes."

He took a deep breath. "I hope you're not feeling *obliged* to be friendly in this fashion with me because of the . . ." He searched for the word. "The 'unpleasantness' that passed between us last year, which you should know actually means very little to me."

"Oh, it means very little?"

"Well, it means something, of course. We can't just ignore it. That would be wrong. It must be accounted for, naturally. I must be compensated, in one way or another. It's only right."

Cowardly bastard, she thought. "No, I don't feel obliged, Mr. Blaisedale."

"Theodore," he reminded her.

"Tell me, Theodore, where would you take me?"

"Once I went to an inn that sits on a bluff in Sausalito."

"What's it called?"

"Ashfield House. I was there with my . . ." He stopped.

Yes, his wife. Good. But what kind of woman would marry a man such as this? She did not care to contemplate the answer. "What's the inn look like?"

"It's painted white with a wide porch that surrounds it."

"And the rooms?"

"They're nice."

"'Nice'? You can do better than that. Make me feel I'm there now. You won't be disappointed."

"You'll come over to me when you're ready?"

"Yes," she said.

He laughed and glanced down to his lap. "I'm already ready, if you know what I mean."

"Please, Theodore. Slow down."

"Okay, let's see . . ." He took a deep breath. "All right, there's a particularly nice guest room that's painted sky blue. It has a view of the sea. And on the walls are paintings of old sailing ships."

"I'm starting to see it." He had taken the bait—now she need only reel him in. She reached across the desk and took his damp hand in hers. "Do they serve food at the inn?" she asked.

"The lamb chops are cooked to perfection."

"Are chops your favorite?"

He nodded. "And in the afternoons they serve tea in antique Chinese cups," he added.

"Do you take your tea with cream and sugar?"

"Why do you ask?"

"I want to know how you like to be served."

"Yes, cream and sugar."

"And the bed?"

"Brass," he said. "With linen sheets and velvet coverlets."

She shook her head no. "I mean, what do you like in the bed?"

"That's a little personal."

"Isn't that the point?"

"I like the usual, I guess."

She smiled. "Come now, a man in an unusual business like yours . . . There must be something unique."

He shrugged.

"Tell me," she pressed. "After all, I'm here to make amends, remember? No sense merely going halfway."

He lowered his voice almost to a whisper. "Well, I like to be called Tom. Yeah, that's a real good name."

"Okay, Tom. That's easy enough."

"I don't mean in ordinary circumstances."

"You mean in intimate moments?"

He nodded.

It was not the strangest request she had ever heard.

"Tom Mix," he continued.

"Like the cowboy star?"

He smiled, his teeth prominent.

She was almost intrigued enough to press for more intimate details— but she had enough now for her purposes and she recalled that her father advised never pushing a mark for the mere sake of entertainment. "Oh yes, I remember now," she said, withdrawing her hands from his.

"What do you mean, 'remember'?"

She stood, gathering her handbag and stepping away from the desk. "I remember that afternoon we spent in one another's arms. I imagine you never told your wife about it."

"What afternoon?"

"It'd be terrible for her if she found out what happened between us last year," she continued. "And in the same sky blue bedroom the two of you once occupied, right? But it was so romantic, how can I keep it a secret? Yes, and you're very passionate too. At least you were with me. Of course, I was underage at the time of our tryst. Legally speaking. But I wasn't so young as to have forgotten the sky blue walls, the lamb chops, the tea cups, or the brass bed."

"You wouldn't."

"I'll be going now," she said.

He stood from behind his desk. "My wife would never believe I was unfaithful."

She pointed to the bulge in his pants.

He sat down once more.

"Mightn't she wonder how I've come to know all that I know about you, *Tom*?" she asked.

He did not answer.

She could walk out the door now. He would make no telephone calls to the police. But Rita had been raised to believe that *breaking even* was only for saps. "I think it'd be a fine gesture if you gave me cab fare," she said. "Actually, it's the only gentlemanly thing to do."

He struggled for words. None came.

"I'm not leaving without cab fare," she continued. Assuming he had no gun in his desk, she'd be all right. He wasn't the sort of man to strike a woman with his fists (though one could never be sure).

"Where is your sense of honor, Miss Gaspereaux?"

"Honor?" She almost laughed. "That's a lovely sentiment."

"It's more than mere sentiment," he snapped. "Honor is what separates human beings from base animals."

"Isn't it also what married people vow to one another?"

He reached into his pants pocket and withdrew a handful of one-dollar bills, tossing them onto his desk.

She did not take the money. "That'll only get me back to my hotel," she said. "I meant cab fare all the way to Hollywood."

He looked at her in disbelief.

"Didn't I tell you that's where I'm going?" she asked.

After a moment, he reached into his suit coat pocket, withdrawing his wallet. He took from it a twenty-dollar bill and set it on the desk.

"Twenty bucks?" She took the money. "Okay. It'll have to do."

"You'll get yours someday," he said.

"Yes, but you won't be the one to give it to me." And she was out the door.

He shouted something after her, but he did not follow.

Outside, she thought of her father—he'd have laughed at her for blundering into a former mark. At his own funeral, of all places! Next, he'd have complimented her for having turned the circumstances to her favor. Finally, he'd have beaten her to remind her of her place. But Cletus Gaspereaux did not laugh at her and he did not compliment her and he did not beat her because he was dead.

She hailed a cab.

"Where to?" the cabbie asked as she climbed in.

She had one more stop to make before getting out of town. "The Hall of Justice, please."

The cabbie nodded and pulled away from the curb. "You want me to drop you on the courthouse side or the jail side?"

"Jail."

She saw his eyebrows rise in the rear-view mirror.

"You got friends there?" he asked.

"That's my business."

"A nice girl like you?"

She shrugged.

"They must be innocent," he said. "Plenty of good people get rail-roaded."

"Yeah, sure." Emil Madrid and Moira O'Shea were likely both gallows bound.

Too bad for them.

Shortly thereafter, the cabbie announced: "The Hall of Justice is over there," negotiating the traffic outside the only building in the city that could justify a name of such preposterous pomposity. He pulled to the curb. The fare was sixty-five cents. Rita opened her handbag. She sorted past the envelope that held the last of her father's cash, which she had found hidden in the suite before the police ransacked the place; then she sorted past the silver and the one-dollar bills that were scattered in her handbag among tubes of lipstick, an eye-liner pencil, her shiny compact, and a dozen hard candies. At last, she removed the twenty-dollar bill she had acquired from Blaisedale. She reached over the front seat and handed it up to the cabbie.

"Hey, I don't have change for that," he said, shaking his head. "You think I'm made of money?"

"I don't have anything smaller," she lied.

"What the hell?"

"I'm sorry but I'm rather disorganized today," she explained. "My father's funeral and all."

"Your father?"

"Yes."

"Oh, that's why you're dressed all in black?"

She nodded.

"Ah, well forget it then Miss. The ride's on me."

"Yeah?"

"You just take care of yourself, young lady."

She patted his shoulder. "What a kind gesture in a wicked world."

❖

Less than an hour after Rita left the mortuary, she and a silent group of men and women followed an armed marshal down a long, windowless corridor. They passed through a steel reinforced doorway and entered a brightly lit room as large as a tennis court; the room was divided at its center by a wire mesh grill that stretched twenty feet from the floor to the ceiling. On the far side of the grill stood two dozen men in denim work clothes. Inmates. Above them, armed guards patrolled a catwalk. "Twenty minutes," said a voice over a public address system. The inmates moved toward the grill—on Rita's side, attorneys, wives, friends, criminal associates, and whoever else had come to visit the inmates did the same. Rita was familiar with the procedure. She had experienced it from both sides of the grill. She found that being on this side afforded one little more respect from the guards than being on the other. The general belief here was that everyone was a crook, whether he or she had been assigned an inmate number or not. Rita did not mind—her experience of human nature inclined her to agree with the sentiment.

She saw Emil Madrid before he saw her.

It was odd to see him wearing prison garb. Ordinarily, Emil was a natty dresser. One never saw him without a fresh flower in his lapel. Now, he hadn't even a lapel. Rita almost laughed. The ill-fitting jail-house clothing made his body appear smaller and stranger than it ordinarily appeared—which was small and strange indeed. But his demeanor was not changed; for example, he was just now talking ani-matedly to a handsome inmate who couldn't be a day over twenty, young enough to be Emil's son. Rita pitied the young man. Emil looked harmless enough, but he was energetic, persistent, and he knew what he wanted. He would wear the poor guy down. Rita had seen it before. Emil had some sort of mysterious way with certain young men.

"Emil!" she called.

He turned and nodded to her, then whispered something to his new friend and started toward the grill. "Ah Rita, my little flower," he said, his strange accent unmistakable among the dozens of voices speaking around them.

Rita moved to the grill; she stood beside a well-dressed attorney almost six and a half feet tall. He was talking through the grating to his client, a local gang boss whose face Rita recognized from the newspapers.

"I was so worried I could hardly sleep," Emil continued, sidling up to the grill beside the gangster. He leaned toward Rita until his face nearly touched the grill. "Yes, I was worrying all night about you, my dear."

"Worried I wouldn't come?" she asked.

Emil looked sheepishly away. "Actually, I was worried that you might not like me anymore, my dear girl."

"Oh, my feelings for you haven't changed."

"Good."

"I've never liked you, Emil."

He looked as if his feelings were hurt. "How can you say that to me?" he asked. "I've been like an uncle to you, Rita. Why, allow me to remind you that I never laid a hand on you, in anger or . . . in that other way."

"That 'other way'?" she asked. "The only reason you never touched me is that I'm a girl."

"How can you dislike me so, my flower?"

"How do I dislike thee?" she started. "Let me count the ways . . ."

He brushed her words away with his hand. "Please, my being in here is no joke. They've got me on a murder charge!"

She shrugged.

"I didn't kill anybody," he said.

"You're implicated."

"I had nothing to do with your father's killing."

"No, that was Wilbur's idea," she said.

"Yes, quite spontaneous of him. Impetuous. Ill-advised. But murders are always taking place. The world is no Garden of Eden, my dear."

She said nothing.

"Besides," he continued, "failing to be my brother's keeper does not make me a murderer."

"The state of California may disagree."

"What does a state know?"

"It knows how to operate a gallows."

"I need your help, Rita."

She should not have come, she thought. Why had she even bothered? Had she come to gloat? No. She didn't *want* to see him executed or imprisoned. But she could offer him nothing. Was there something he could offer her? No. He was beaten. Yet here she was. Why? Was it because everyone else she had ever known was gone now? Was it because he was all she had left, even if he was no good? She didn't like to think of herself as being weak in that way. But she could arrive at no better answer.

"I need money for a good attorney," he continued. "And then my attorney will need more money to grease a few important palms. San Francisco is not the least corrupt city in the world, my dear. Do you understand? But to move its machinery, one must have cash. A man of my highly cultured disposition will wilt like a rose in here if left untended."

"You'll be well tended in there."

"You don't understand!" he shouted. "Why does no one understand?"

"Please, Emil, calm down."

He lowered his voice. "They've got nothing on me but circumstantial evidence. Do you understand? I must have a good attorney!" He gestured to the attorney at Rita's side. "Like that one there."

The tall attorney glanced away from his client and turned to Emil.

The gang boss did the same from his side of the grill, placing one hand on Emil's shoulder: "This is a private conversation, understand little guy?"

Emil turned back to Rita. "Do you see how misunderstood I am in here?"

"You're misunderstood everywhere, Emil."

"Tell me, how was your father's service?"

"It was not well attended."

"Who was there?"

"Just me and the detective."

"Hammett?"

She nodded. Hammett had shaken her hand and offered a brief condolence after the service. He was tall and thin with prematurely gray hair. He looked fragile of health, but he was hard in his manner and Rita found him attractive.

"And the funeral?" Emil asked.

She shook her head no. "He's being cremated."

"I'd have been there, you know. Offering my respects. If only I were free."

Emil was always afraid of her father—with good reason. Cletus Gaspereaux was a formidable enemy, if crossed. Ordinarily, Emil might even have felt relieved to have Gaspereaux removed from the scene. But now, behind bars, he doubtless would have appreciated a bit of her father's advice and influence. "I almost made a mess of it," she said.

"How?"

"It turns out this was not the first time this particular undertaker buried my 'father.'"

"He'd been a mark?"

She nodded. "I'd forgotten him."

"What did you do?"

"I conversed with him and in the end he shared a little too much information for his own good."

"Oh? Married?"

She nodded.

Emil laughed.

"My father would have laughed too."

"Yes, and then he'd have . . ." He stopped. There was no need to finish. Both knew how it worked.

"Yes, he would have."

"He could be a most difficult man."

"Always."

"Still, it's a tough break for him," Emil said. "Gunned down by his
own bodyguard . . ." He shook his head as if discouraged by the state of
the world. "Of course, Cletus was no innocent. You should have seen
how willing he was to give Wilbur up when that brute Sam Hammett
suggested the police would need a fall guy."

"That's true, my father was no innocent."

"He was no father to you."

She shrugged.

"What will you do now that he's gone?" he asked.

"I'm getting out of the rackets, Emil."

He looked at her, disbelieving.

"I mean it," she continued.

"You can't mean it, my dear. It's impossible."

"Why?"

He grinned. "Because you may take the girl out of the rackets, but
you'll never take the rackets out of the girl."

"That's a little too clever, Emil."

"It seems clever to you only because it's true."

"Tomorrow, I'm going to Hollywood to be a motion picture actress."

His expression darkened. "You can't be serious."

"I am."

He pulled back, as if the news dealt him a blow. "But what of my
years of hard work?"

"Hard work?"

"Teaching you the angles."

She said nothing.

"My dear," he continued. "Your education has been my primary concern from the beginning."

She almost laughed.

"Motion pictures cannot possibly be your true calling," he continued. "Why, you've already found your calling, Rita. Or rather, your late father and I found it for you. We took you from an orphanage and raised you to heights undreamed of! Remember?"

"These are depths, not heights."

"This is just one moment in a lifetime of moments. Have you forgotten all the others that have come before?"

"I've forgotten very little," she said. "Unfortunately."

"But you're our masterpiece. It would break your father's heart. And mine too."

"You have a heart, Emil?"

"You needn't thank me for all I've taught you," he said. "But please don't make light of a broken-hearted man."

"Acting for a camera and conning a mark isn't so different."

"But movie people are no better than circus people!"

"And what of the people we've traveled among?"

"We only ever gave them what they deserved, my delicate blossom. None of them would have been marks in the first place if it weren't for their avarice. That's the difference. We are people with a mission."

"Like avenging angels?"

"Yes, exactly."

"You're mad, Emil."

"We made you what you are today, my dear."

He was not wrong in this, she thought. And that was the problem. "I didn't come here for your blessing."

He drew nearer the metal grill. "What did you come for?"

Yes, good question. "To say goodbye, I suppose."

"Because you like me?" he asked.

"I never liked you, Emil."

He studied her face. After a moment, he grinned. "You might make a fine screen actress, after all."

"Why the change of heart?"

"Because you are quite compelling when you lie," he answered. "Like now. When you said you've never liked me. It was almost convincing."

"Okay, maybe I don't hate you."

"Then do something for me, Rita."

She knew better than to speak.

"I need money," he continued. "Quite a lot of it."

"You're not going to need money where you're going."

"That's just it!" he shouted, his eyes bulging. "They want to kill me!"

"Calm down, Emil."

He lowered his voice. "I need money to get the kind of attorney who can buy jurors and maybe even a judge. Anything can be arranged, you know. But justice does not come cheap in this city."

"You have money."

"Only a few hundred."

"You're lying," she said.

He shook his head no. "About a year ago, I invested in a South African diamond mine that proved to be . . ." He stopped.

"Disappointing?" she asked.

"Nonexistent."

"You were swindled?"

"No one is infallible, my dear."

She laughed.

"Ordinarily," he continued, "I would have no trouble obtaining necessary goods and services, with or without cash in hand. But mine are no longer ordinary circumstances." He lowered his voice. "Judges and prosecutors and jurors can be bought, but only on a cash basis."

"Maybe they'll settle for a deed to the Brooklyn Bridge."

"This is not a joke, Rita!"

"I can't help you with money."

"Look, the only one of us who ever got ahead in this game was the Big Man," he snapped. "He must have put away a fortune."

"Maybe he did, maybe he didn't," she said. "I wouldn't know."

Emil said nothing.

"Do you think he trusted me with his finances?" she asked.

"But surely . . ."

"The truth is, I'm almost broke myself," she continued.

"You're lying."

She had already spent most of the twelve hundred dollars she found hidden among her father's effects after she learned of his murder. She did not know where he had stashed the rest—perhaps in a bank in Zurich, perhaps in a mattress in Detroit, perhaps there was nothing more to stash. "Do you think he left some kind of will?" she continued. "Or a handy little bank book?"

Emil gathered himself. "That's all right, my dear. I know how you can get plenty of money for me."

"I'm not doing any more jobs."

He turned his wide eyes heavenward. "It's not only for myself that I ask you to do this for me."

"No?"

"I'm thinking of you as well. Because after you get me out of here you'll be able to retire from the graft and enter the next phase of your professional life with a clear conscience."

"Conscience?" After all these years, Emil still managed sometimes to amaze her.

"Yes, because only then will you have fulfilled your potential as our protégé . . ." He closed his eyes as if picturing the circumstance. He opened them once more, enthusiastic. "Yes, and *then* you can go to Hollywood and become the next Mary Pickford."

"Tests indicate that I possess a dark mystery that she lacks," she answered. "I'm more a Constance Talmadge."

"Well, whomever."

"But there'll be no swan song, Emil."

"What are you saying?"

"Tomorrow, I'm going to Hollywood."

"Well, regardless of your decision, you're planning to get me out of here first, aren't you?"

She said nothing.

"You must secure my freedom, Rita. Then I can help you with your new career."

"I don't want your help, Emil."

"But my wealth of worldly experience . . ."

"Has landed you here," Rita said.

"Fine," he snapped. "Do what you want with your life. But still you owe me a debt for making you my protégé!"

"You used me, Emil. That's all. Just like my father did."

He ignored her accusation. "My little flower, you don't actually want to see me go to the death house, do you?"

No.

"You don't have to feel family-type feelings for me," Emil continued. "God knows I've been like an uncle to you. But I won't ask you for family-type love."

"Good."

"If you can't love, my dear . . . well, that's quite sad. But it's more your problem than mine."

"Not when they put the rope around your neck."

"Bitch!" he snapped.

She stepped back.

Emil lowered his eyes and caught his breath. "I'm sorry, Rita. I shouldn't have called you names."

"You'd never have dared if my father was alive."

"It's the stress of this place. I'm almost out of my head."

"I'm not incapable of love," she said.

When she was seven or eight years old, she had felt great affection for a puppy she named Beauty. After only a few weeks, however, a Customs official forbade Beauty's entry into one or another of the countries through which Rita and her father passed on business. Her father gave the dog to the Customs official, who attempted to assure Rita (in a language she did not understand) that he would take good care of the puppy. Even now, Rita sometimes wondered if Beauty—who would be more than ten years old—were still alive. And she remembered feeling affection for her friends in the orphanage, though she could no longer recall their faces. And sometimes she had felt affection for her father, despite everything. His laughter was infectious, especially after he'd had a few drinks. But she had long before learned how little such feelings were worth.

"Who do you love?" Emil asked.

"It's 'whom,'" she corrected.

"That's not the point," Emil said.

"Exactly," she snapped. "Love has nothing to do with it."

"I'm asking you for something other than love."

"Yes, money," she said.

He nodded, lowering his voice almost to a whisper. "Of course, I would repay you with information worth far more than whatever financial aid you ultimately provide."

"Information about what?"

"There is a Russian Count," Emil said.

"Keransky?" she asked, recalling that her father had shouted the name a few days before when the Black Falcon proved a fake. Count Keransky.

"Our involvement with the Falcon begins with the Russian," Emil said. "Eighteen years ago."

"I'm not interested in the bird," she said. "It was my father's nightmare, not mine."

He motioned with his index finger for her to draw closer to the grill and spoke in a whisper, pressing his lips so close to the metal that she could feel his breath in her ear: "His nightmare, yes. But for you, a dream."

She laughed. "Who do you think you're dealing with, Emil? A child?"

"A friend."

"Don't count on that."

He looked away, wiping at a tear. "Then I am truly friendless."

She had to admit—the tear was good. The little man had a gift.

"It is true, my dear, that none of us ever treated you properly." He lowered his eyes. "You have every right to be angry. Do you think I am foolish enough not to know that?"

"I think you're wicked enough not to care."

"Maybe I ought not to tell you the truth about the bird," he said.

"I don't give a damn about it."

"But our futures are tied to it!"

"Not my future. And your future, Emil, appears to be tied only to the end of a rope."

"Bitch!" he snapped.

She smiled.

He rubbed his palm over his face. "Your rope imagery is clever but insensitive, my dear," he said. "It set me off. I'm sorry. Still, you're not wrong about my prospects."

She said nothing.

"Do you understand this is no joke?" he pressed. "I'm a goner, unless you help me."

"I told you, I have no money."

"But you've a good mind for graft. And there are many ways to raise quick capital, especially for a girl as attractive and well-versed in the ways of the world as you."

"What are you talking about?"

"Saving my life."

"How?"

"I'm not asking you to do anything you haven't already done many times before. An attractive girl like you, wise to the world. You know a mark when you see one. Why, you could raise three grand in three weeks if you worked it right. A convention, for example."

"What, exactly, are you suggesting?"

"Look, you worked the undertaker without even taking off your clothes."

"Drop dead, Emil."

"Don't play the prude with me," he said.

She turned.

His tone of voice softened. "I could direct you to a supply of laudanum or some other substance to take the edge off. Just as your father did."

"You know about that?" she asked.

"I always admired your team spirit."

As recently as this past Tuesday night, mere hours before their house of cards collapsed in a hail of gunfire, Rita's father had slipped laudanum into her glass of milk. He had done so many times before as a tactic to delay patrolmen, detectives, petty hoods, rival underground "art" collectors, or whoever else might be drawing too near to him, too fast. Around the time of Rita's fourteenth birthday, he had discovered that even the most motivated of his rivals would delay their hottest pursuit when they discovered in his suite not Gaspereaux (who could be elsewhere, doing urgent business) but his pretty young daughter—drugged and alone in a revealing, silk nightgown. The tactic delayed rivals anywhere from thirty minutes to three hours. The most honorable of them, which included the detective Sam Hammett, merely walked the overdosed girl around the suite to keep her from losing consciousness until an ambulance arrived. As for the others, less honorable . . . She remembered only snatches of the encounters—sometimes, she remembered nothing at all. Gaspereaux justified the tactic on the grounds that what one cannot remember might as well not have happened. She didn't mind the laudanum-induced dreams, which were colorful and rich, if sometimes terrifying. However, she sometimes found herself alone for a long time. Too long. That's when she had to find means to keep from falling asleep, which her father had warned her was the one thing she must not do. Cold water did not always work; hot coffee was little better. Sometimes, she had to find sharp objects with which to cut herself.

"I'm finished with that life," she said.

He chuckled. "But that life's not finished with you."

"Go to Hell," she said, turning to go.

"Wait," he called. "I have something you're going to want."

She stopped, but did not turn around.

"It's a simple arrangement," Emil continued. "I'll give it to you when you deliver to my defense fund three thousand dollars, which you may acquire in whatever manner you're able. Such as a cake sale, for instance."

She turned to him. "You have nothing I want."

"Do you recall when I said that Cletus Gaspereaux was no father to you?"

She said nothing.

"I suspect you didn't fully understand me, my dear," Emil continued. "You see, I meant it literally. He was no father to you."

"What?"

"Cletus Gaspereaux was not your father."

She said nothing.

"How could a pretty little thing like you ever have been the fruit of his seed?" he asked.

"That's absurd," she said. But there *had* been times she had studied her own face in the mirror, looking into her eyes for something that might recall her father's eyes. Was that a shared speck of green floating in the darker iris? Yes, she and her father laughed alike—but was that evidence of anything beyond their having lived together for a long time? She suspected the story of Cletus Gaspereaux and Polly Shaw meeting in Times Square was a fabrication; she knew Gaspereaux might not have actually fathered her—after all, she had never known him to go with a woman. She might have been born a common child, orphaned and destitute. So she had never pressed the manner.

"Your real father is still living," Emil said. "Gaspereaux acquired you as an infant and deposited you in the orphanage."

"Stole me?"

"Acquired," Emil said.

"Kidnapped me?" she pressed.

He nodded.

"Why?"

"The usual reason," he answered. "Ransom. But not mere money. Nothing as pedestrian as that."

"Not money? Then what?"

"The Black Falcon, of course."

"I don't follow."

"Your real father possessed the statuette. He still does. You see, he refused to pay the ransom." Emil pointed to Rita's right hand, where her pinkie finger ended at the second joint. "Yes, your real father is a hard man. He refused to make a deal, an exchange, even after he received half of your little baby finger in the mail as a warning. Instead, he changed his identity and disappeared with the Falcon."

Rita shook her head no. "I lost the tip of this finger in an accident."

"Oh, is that what they told you at the orphanage?"

"That's what everyone's always told me. You know that."

"Well, don't feel too bad. At least Gaspereaux didn't follow through with his threat to kill you while you were an infant. You can be thankful for that, my dear. Of course, you were useless to him at that time. What interest had he in diapers and midnight feedings? So the orphanage took his money and raised you as one of theirs until he returned to reclaim you at age five. Doubtless, you remember that as the start of your new life. Gaspereaux believed having a daughter would prove useful to him as he grew older. In this, of course, he was right."

"I don't believe you, Emil. I'll contact the orphanage."

"I'm afraid not, my dear. The orphanage burned down a few weeks after your father claimed you. Arson. The culprits were never apprehended. What a tragedy. All the records were lost in the blaze. Which is to say nothing of many children."

She said nothing.

"In your heart you know it's true," he said.

She did not know what she knew in her heart. "How do you know this is so, Emil?"

"It was Moira and I who acquired you."

"From my real father?"

Emil nodded, sheepishly. "I've been in the employ of Cletus Gaspereaux for a long time, my dear. I make no apologies. Everyone has to work for a living. That's why I believe the word 'acquire' describes what we do in our business far better than words like 'steal' or 'kidnap.' 'Stealing' a child is a gross act, but 'acquiring' one is merely a job. "

"*Our* business?" Rita asked. "I'm not like you, Emil. I'm no kidnapper."

"Rita, you've no idea what you are," he answered. "Or what you've been. All the small parts you've played in your father's larger schemes . . . Why do you think he kept you ignorant of the way his plans really worked? Oh yes, you've been an accessory to kidnapping, Rita. Whether you knew it or not. And worse."

"You bastard, Emil."

"Don't be angry at me, my dear. Why, look at the fascinating adventures we've given you over the years."

"I hope they kill you."

"It's only growing pains you're feeling, my little tea rose. You don't really want me to die."

"So you're saying this Russian count is my real father?" she asked.

Emil shrugged playfully, as if he didn't know the answer to her question.

"Where is he?" she asked.

Emil smiled. "Now do you see how our little arrangement is going to work?"

"I'll go across the street to the women's jail," she said. "I'll ask Moira. She'll tell me if what you're saying is true. She'll fill me in."

"She can't tell you."

"I'll strike a better bargain with her."

"She hanged herself last night, my dear."

"What?"

"Yes."

"How do you know?"

"Word travels fast in here."

She said nothing.

"And if the state executes me," he continued, "you'll have to live the rest of your life never knowing where to find your true father."

"Do you think I'm some kind of fool?"

"To the contrary, I think you're a brilliant judge of character."

"And I judge your character to be corrupt."

"Indeed it is. I am a cheat and a liar. But that doesn't mean I am cheating or lying to you now, my dear."

Rita thought for a moment. Then she shook her head no. "Even if what you're saying is true, why would I care about this Russian? If he was unwilling to trade a statuette for the life of his own child . . . well, he's no father to me. He's nothing to me. I've had enough of all that garbage. So why would I seek him out?"

"Revenge," Emil proposed.

"No." Gaspereaux had always preached that vengeance was strictly for suckers. Rita agreed.

"Better yet, you'd seek him out to acquire the statuette," Emil said.

"I told you, Emil. I don't give a damn about the black bird."

"I can help you acquire a fortune, my little dove. If only you'll help me."

"Keep your secrets. I'm truly not interested." She turned and started away.

"Rita, wait!" he called. "Rita. Come back!"

She continued out of the holding area, through the security checkpoint and out onto the sidewalk, where she walked away from the Hall of Justice. She should never have come, she thought. What had she expected from Emil? But that didn't matter now. She was finished with it. All of it. Some Russian was her true father? Unlikely story. And even if it were true, so what? She was eighteen years old. She didn't need parenting anymore. Actually, she had never needed it. Or, if she had, it was too late to seek it now. And vengeance *was* strictly for suckers. The Falcon was an abomination. Hollywood was the answer. There, she would remake herself as she saw fit. Unfortunately, these consuming thoughts took her two blocks from the Hall of Justice before she realized she'd left her handbag on the floor in the jail among the other visitors.

She raced back, but visiting hours were over.

The guards told her the bag and its contents were gone.

Her last four hundred and sixty-two dollars.

CHAPTER TWO

Rita did not spend her last night in San Francisco as she had planned. She did not change into one of her brightly colored dresses and go to a nightclub in the manner she had day-dreamed about doing since she was a child—alone, independent, and no longer having to suffer a father who pointed across the dance floor to tell her which man to approach with which of her practiced remarks. She had thought tonight she might choose a man simply because she liked "the cut of his jib" (as her father would have expressed it). Or perhaps allow a man to choose her. Or maybe just settle into a booth alone and enjoy the nightclub's orchestra and the graceful service of the mustachioed waiters in their cutaway coats and white gloves. But she did none of these things. Rather, after she left Madrid in the Hall of Justice she pawned her wristwatch and her opal ring for fifty-two dollars, then wandered the streets downtown until almost dark, at which time she took a cab to the Embarcadero, settling on a bench and watching passengers board and disembark from the ferries. Each passenger seemed to have some important place to go. Strange, she thought. How could there be an important place for each? When she got hungry she bought a bowl of fish chowder and took it back to her bench.

Was it her fault that she had a talent for dissemination?

Or that her attractiveness to men made her useful in confidence games?

Or that she had a taste for such games, with their menace and excitement and payoff?

In the past two months she and Gaspereaux had traveled by train from Rome to Athens, where they had boarded the first in a series of ships that carried them across the Mediterranean and through the Suez Canal, out the Red Sea and across the Indian Ocean, with stops in Manila and Singapore before arriving in Hong Kong—where who knew what had happened between Gaspereaux and the Chinese contact who handled the smuggling into San Francisco of what eventually proved to be the counterfeit Falcon? All that was over. As Gaspereaux himself was over. And now Emil had given Rita something else to think about. The Russian. Her real father. Likely a lie, of course. But what if it were true? What might a normal girl be feeling now? Rita hoped these hours would supply an answer. But around ten o'clock, when the wind off the bay grew too cold to tolerate and she still felt absolutely nothing, she stood up from the bench and gave up.

Her hotel suite was silent.

There, she draped her jacket over a chair and moved to the window. Moonlight bathed the hills of the city. The world was full of ghosts tonight, she thought. But what was one to do? Two nights before, she had ransacked her father's belongings in hopes of finding the stash of laudanum he had drawn upon for years to ease her nights. However, the police had taken it away. She did not much like alcohol. So, she turned her attention to the novel she had bought a few days before in North Beach.

Fiction was almost as effective an escape as laudanum.

She liked the book, even if it was soft in parts. Perhaps she liked it *because* it was soft, she thought. Real life provided enough hardness. Why turn to fiction for something that was already all around? And she liked this novel, *Dorothy G., Kansas* more than most others because it followed the adventures of an eighteen-year-old girl who was very little like her. Nothing like her, really. An innocent, a naïf. More intriguing yet, this main character was supposed to be Dorothy Gale from *The Wizard of Oz*, grown now to young adulthood. As in the children's book, Dorothy had returned to Kansas. But this story begins years after her adventures in Oz, as the now-eighteen-year-old Dorothy leaves

Aunt Em and Uncle Henry's farm to embark on a second journey of exploration—this one in the real world, absent any yellow brick road or other fantastical elements, but adventurous nonetheless. Rita thought it a brilliant conceit. After all, any girl who has been to the Emerald City is bound to want to leave Kansas sooner or later, however much she may at first have claimed there was "no place like home." No place? Try New York or Paris. Cities as wondrous in their ways as Oz. Yes, at times the Dorothy character struck Rita as clueless, particularly among the cosmopolitans. But this grown version of Dorothy was not stupid. And oh what a blessing to be clueless, Rita thought. What an enviable privilege.

She opened the book and picked up where she had left off in chapter two.

❖

The first thing Dorothy noticed as she stepped into Harold Burke's apartment was that his floors were painted black.

Very aesthetic, she thought.

The air smelled of cigarettes, the butts of which remained piled in a half dozen tin ash trays that were scattered among books, writing pads, sketches, and unwashed clothing on the black floor. Canvases of swirling colors—paint sometimes as thick as a man's thumb—hung on the gray walls. The paintings were very different from the small drawing Dorothy had brought with her. She knew only enough to recognize them as being "post post-impressionism," whatever that meant; nonetheless, she loved their vitality and, more, their disregard for techniques (particularly perspective) that two years before she had failed to master in her high school art class. Now, she moved deeper into the room. Harold closed the door behind them. A writing desk and chair stood beside a stove. A wardrobe stood in another corner. Dorothy stepped past Harold's narrow, unmade bed to the room's only window. Smaller than any of the canvases, the window opened onto the moonlit street below, where red brick buildings ran in a crazy grid all the way from Fourteenth Street to Battery Park.

"What do you think, Dorothy?"

"It's you," she answered. "Yes. It's perfect."

Dorothy had first seen Harold Burke, the forty-three-year-old artist and critic, three weeks before at the Proper Pagan Tea Room on Sixth Street. At that time, she was still living in Midtown Manhattan at the Wellington, where she had "crash-landed" after her year-and-a-half of wandering from the farm in Kansas through Chicago (where she had stayed with cousins), across the Atlantic with her urbane Aunt Sylvia to visit the attractions in Michelin's Guide to Europe, and then back to the States—specifically, to New York City, where she had hoped to study literature at Columbia. Greenwich Village had never been part of Dorothy's plans. Nonetheless, on her first afternoon in New York she traveled downtown to visit her friend Nancy Bing, whom she and Aunt Sylvia had met the year before in Italy. Nancy—a short, round native of Philadelphia—had been studying painting in Florence. There, she and Dorothy had toured the Uffizi and later strolled the banks of the Arno. Now, Nancy Bing waited tables in the Village, a place she described in her letters to Dorothy (whose European tour continued long past Nancy's return to the States) as being more inspiring to the modern artist than the "sanctified mausoleums of old, old Italy."

"Well, look who's here!" Nancy Bing called the first time Dorothy walked into the tea room.

The small restaurant and its eight tables were lit by dozens of candles, some set on the black tablecloths, others hung on wrought-iron chandeliers, others stacked in the corners, one atop another, like dripping, leaning towers. The wooden floor was thick with hardened wax that crunched beneath one's feet.

Dorothy loved it.

Within a week, she had moved her luggage out of the Wellington

and into a single room above the Proper Pagan, where she began waiting tables with Nancy six days a week. Aunt Sylvia would never have
approved of the broken-down, cold-water flat. Or the job. But that
didn't matter anymore. Dorothy was no longer engaged in a respectable
tour of popular European tourist attractions. All that had failed her,
she thought. Hadn't she undertaken the tour to gain experience otherwise unobtainable in places like Kansas or even in Chicago, Boston, or
New York? Wasn't that the trip's whole *raison d'être*? But in the end,
Dorothy believed she had learned little more from her eighteen months
abroad than she'd have learned by reading a well-illustrated travel guide.

Here in the Village everything seemed new to Dorothy. The buildings dated from the early nineteenth century, but inside the totter-
ing brick structures Dorothy found what she thought of as the *present*. Nancy had been right. Here, up cement stoops and behind brick
facades, were studios where color and music and literature came into
being from nothing more than paint and canvas, ink, and paper. How
could enrolling in college match up to this? Sometimes, she wondered
what her Aunt Em would make of these new experiences. In her letters
home Dorothy tried to describe her life. By the curtness of Aunt Em's
replies, however, she knew that she failed to express her experiences
adequately. Perhaps she did not believe her niece's exuberance, Dorothy
thought. Perhaps her letters home were unbalanced, like poorly written
essays. All emotion, unsubstantiated. Of course, no place is perfect—no
experience purely blissful. So she wrote to her aunt of the single frustration that dogged her first weeks in the Village, a frustration that she had
not mentioned even to Nancy:

"I can't help but wonder what it feels like not only to admire artistic
creations but to actually create," she wrote. "What does it feel like to be
one with the creation itself, if only for a moment? When the tip of the
brush touches the canvas, for example, and beauty or terror emerges. I
wonder and I wish. Believe me, I've tried. My friend Nancy is generous
with her supplies and her encouragement. But nothing ever happens for

me. I paint mush. And aside from further wishing, I don't know what else to do to gain so lofty a goal. I mean, I understand that artists are not made by mere wishing. It's hard work, right? Like everything else. Isn't that what you always taught me? But it's not work alone, Auntie Em, and I don't think I have inside of me that other 'something' that being an artist seems to require . . ."

To which she replied:

"Your uncle and I worry and wonder what is <u>becoming</u> of you! Girl-hood fantasies of magical lands are one thing, dear Dorothy, particularly when they are the result of a mortal scare from a battering tornado. Weren't we always understanding about your recovery all those years ago? Indeed we were. But this is something different. You've no excuses now for flightiness!"

Dorothy was disappointed, but not surprised. "I'll tell you what's becoming of me!" she scribbled in a letter that she never mailed. "My nights are filled with talk and cigarettes and bootleg whiskey and sex, sex, sex!"

The talk, cigarettes, and whiskey were true.

As for the sex:

"You've never even necked?" Nancy Bing asked late one night in her studio apartment. She was painting one of her bold, confusing pictures (*Vital Source,* she called it) as Dorothy lounged in a torn leather chair across the room, chain-smoking cigarettes, watching each stroke of Nancy's brush.

"Oh, I've been kissed," Dorothy answered. "By more than one boy."

Nancy put down her brush. "Kissing and necking are not the same thing."

"My boyfriend in high school was very passionate, really," Dorothy continued. She took a long drag on her cigarette. "Ned . . . He always wanted to hold my hand in public, as if we were engaged or something. Once, in church, he put his hand on my knee, right where the Minister himself could have seen it if he had glanced over at the right moment."

"That doesn't exactly make you Theda Bara."

"So. Who wants to be Theda Bara anyway?"

"Everyone," Nancy said.

Dorothy shrugged in agreement.

"Aren't you curious?" Nancy asked.

"Of course."

"Why don't you do something about it, Dorothy?"

"About 'necking'?"

"That's a place to start."

Dorothy stood up, setting her cigarette in an ashtray. "Fine, Nancy. If you must know, I've never actually heard the word before. So who knows, maybe I've necked before but I just don't know it. Maybe I've done it a thousand times. It's just that nobody ever said anything about 'necking' back in Kansas. Still, there's nothing new under the sun, right? I mean, maybe it's just a matter of semantics."

"Oh, you'd know, if you'd done it."

"All right, all right, what the hell is 'necking'?"

Nancy put down her brush and crossed the room to her friend. She put her hands on Dorothy's shoulders, pulling her close. Then closer.

Dorothy laughed. "What are you doing?"

Nancy placed her lips—parted, moist—beneath Dorothy's chin. Dorothy's body tightened. "Relax," Nancy whispered. Dorothy took a deep breath; Nancy ran her lips slowly along the line of Dorothy's jaw all the way up to the base of Dorothy's ear, where she lingered for a moment, her breaths warm. She stepped back. "That's necking," she said.

For a moment neither spoke.

"It's nice," Dorothy said at last. "But kind of slobbery."

Nancy laughed and returned to her painting.

"So, you do that to men?" Dorothy asked.

"As many as I can," Nancy answered. "That and other things."

"What a devil you are!"

"Hey, 'there's nothing either right or wrong, but thinking makes it so,'" Nancy said. "That's Shakespeare."

"Hmmm..."

"Half the men in the Village want to date you, Dorothy. Don't you know that?"

"What!"

"That's how it is, my friend."

"Oh, I don't think so."

"Dorothy, I think it's time you opened your eyes."

She merely laughed.

"I mean it," Nancy continued. "Tomorrow at work look around you. See the way men look at you."

"Okay, okay..."

"You know, it's all right to look back at them, once in a while."

"Oh, I do."

"Sure..." Nancy answered.

Dorothy had begun to look around her at the Proper Pagan. There, her eyes had already discovered Harold Burke, who was unlike anyone she had ever known. His paintings were well known in the Village and his art reviews and essays appeared in journals that included *The Broom* and *The Dial*. He was tall, like Dorothy's uncle, and though he was twice her age, his eyes shined with a casual mischief that captured and held her attention in ways it had never been held before. At first, she didn't understand. In Kansas, Ned had sometimes asked her to gaze for long periods into his hungry teenage eyes (he called it "mooning"). She always obliged him, but never failed to feel silly rather than amorous. Harold did not have to ask for attention. He was graceful and stylish, even in a paint-splattered jacket and worn boots. A man among boys, she thought. He did not speak much, but when he did, whomever he spoke to listened (art-world rivals included).

Sometimes, even those who were not with him listened as well.

Before making his acquaintance, Dorothy eavesdropped on his

conversations whenever she served him. The first words she ever heard him speak had been addressed to a younger artist with whom he drank coffee one night long past midnight: "If you're painting the war," he said, "then your canvas should be splattered with paint, unceremoniously, as the ground there was splattered with blood. Anything else is pretension or denial, which is the antithesis of art. By God, the loosened, pumping arteries of those dying boys knew how to express war, right there on the cracked ground of France. Who are you to try to express otherwise with your carefully drafted lines and art-schooled shadings!" Such words thrilled Dorothy. Even Nancy Bing did not say such things. She could not. She had not been "over there." Harold had. The Great War. And he had experienced it all with the eyes of a real artist—a status that had first been confirmed almost twenty years before by the success of his early shows, which everyone in the tea room knew had been described by the *Times*, the *World*, and the *American Mercury* as "very promising..."

Dorothy loved to watch the way his large hands picked up a coffee cup.

Then one afternoon—not long after Nancy showed Dorothy how to neck—Harold Burke spoke to Dorothy with more than his customary courtesy. He was sitting alone. She had delivered to him his cup of coffee, which he always drank black. She expected him to say thank you. Instead, he said: "You know, you're a flower growing in the mud."

She did not know how to respond. "I like mud, I guess," she said, at last. Immediately, she felt stupid, which was not a common feeling for Dorothy.

"I've been watching you," he continued. "Can you sit with me?"

The tea room was slow. "Okay." She set her tray full of porcelain cups on the table.

"My name is Harold."

"Oh yes, I know."

"And yours?"

"Dorothy."

He sipped his coffee. "Hmmm. Very nice. But you seem more like a 'Carrie' to me."

"Oh, why?" She was not pleased. "You mean I remind you of a strong person, like Carrie Nation?"

He shrugged then pointed to her tray. "Actually, I meant it like *carry* coffee."

"Oh, of course." Was he making fun of her? Nonetheless, she laughed, uncertain what else to do.

"I'm sorry," he said, grinning. "It's an idiotic thing for me to say, but you have the most amazing balance with that tray and those cups. I've never seen you spill a drop. Sometimes it's like a wonderful circus act."

"Oh, I've spilled plenty."

"No, I think you're just being modest."

She didn't know what to say. Truth was, she hadn't ever spilled a drop.

"Where are you from?" he asked.

"Kansas."

"Ah, garden spot of the nation."

She laughed.

"Originally, I'm from Rochester, Minnesota," he continued. "Not exactly the vital center of Western culture either. But . . . Here we are, you and me, Midwesterners far from our homes, and look at what we've become."

"And what have we become?" Dorothy asked.

"Tablemates."

"That's not bad."

"For a beginning," he said.

"And what comes after tablemates?"

"Friends," he answered. "Can I buy you a coffee?"

"That's a very nice offer," she answered. "But, since I'm the waitress here, does that mean I'd have to get it myself?"

He smiled, stood, and moved to the swinging doors that separated the kitchen from the dining room. He disappeared inside, re-emerging a moment later with the coffee. He returned to the table and set the cup before Dorothy.

"Thank you," she said.

Nancy Bing followed Harold out of the kitchen, her hands wet from washing dishes. She winked at Dorothy and then disappeared back through the swinging doors.

"What do you think, do I have a future as a waiter?" he asked.

She gathered her courage. "Well, *I'd* leave you a nice tip," she answered. "Of course, not all customers are as soft-hearted as me."

He took a small notebook from his jacket pocket and a pencil from behind his ear. He jotted something in the book.

"What are you writing?"

"I'm noting the first two things I ever learned about you."

"Which are?"

"That you're from Kansas," he said, returning the book to his pocket and sitting down. "And that you're soft-hearted."

"But not soft-headed."

"Of course not."

"No, please, write that down too, 'soft-hearted, but not soft-headed.'"

He laughed.

"No, really. Write it."

"All right." He took the book once more from his pocket and noted her words. "There. Feel better?"

"Much."

"Are you a budding artist?" he asked.

She shook her head no.

"Playwright, novelist?"

"No." She looked away. "I mean, I like all those things very much . . ."

"Thank God," he interrupted, leaning back in his chair. "It's refresh-

ing to meet someone who's not like everybody else around here. You
know, aspiring artists who don't know what the hell they're really doing,
who put more time into selecting the proper wardrobe than actually
practicing their craft, who chatter and talk like experts but choke up
altogether with a brush or a pen in their hand. I swear, they outnumber
the rats in the Village. Damn dilettantes. Aspiration is choking the air
out of these streets. Some days I can barely breathe, by God! An honest day's work—that's what makes air breathable. How fine for you to
just be the person you are, without need of a portfolio to justify your
existence. I swear to God, being a waitress is the finest profession in the
world."

What a speech! she thought. "Harold, I'm not really a waitress," she
said.

"No?"

She thought fast. She leaned forward, motioning with her finger for
him to draw nearer. "Truth is," she whispered. "I'm a detective."

He grinned. "Like Sherlock Holmes?"

She shook her head no. "I'm afraid I can't say any more about it.
Many lives depend upon my silence."

He laughed. "Oh, well in that case . . ."

But she did not laugh. She did not even smile.

He stopped. "Are you kidding?" he asked.

She said nothing.

"Well, life is full of little mysteries, isn't it?" he said.

She felt her heart pounding. "Big mysteries too," she said.

He slid a calling card across the table. His address. "Look, for all
its mysteries, life is very short. Will you come see me tonight, Carrie?"

"My name is Dorothy." She took the card. "And I don't know if
you'll see me tonight."

"Nine o'clock," he continued. "I have a little apartment here. Nothing fancy. But that doesn't matter to you, does it?"

"Fanciness? Oh, of course not."

"Well then, will you come?"

"For drinks?"

"For whatever," he answered

"My, you are forward, Mr. Harold Burke." She liked saying his name.

"Look, I'm sorry." He sipped his coffee. "I can see you're a very nice girl. I understand. Niceness is, well, nice. The bedrock of a stable society, right? Everyone to his or her proscribed place. Not to mention all that religious stuff. But I've seen things in the last few years that convinced me life is too short for niceties. I like you, Carrie. It's that simple. I'm sorry, but I don't believe in nineteenth-century values. Courtship as property management. Sometimes I wish I could. But I'm modern, whether I like it or not. Do you understand?"

She felt disoriented by the speed of it all—as she had felt as a girl on the downward slopes of the roller coaster at Palace Park. Thrilled, but slightly nauseous.

"And you're modern too," he continued.

Was this how things were done around here? Dorothy knew what her aunt and uncle would have her say. No, no. But then, what was Dorothy to make of the fact that even now Harold's gaze cast a delicious glow that made her feel warm inside. Wasn't that warmth worth considering?

"Oh, Carrie, Carrie, don't look so serious about it."

She took a deep breath.

He smiled and patted her hand. "Whatever you decide is all right. It's only love, only life. You can't make a wrong decision, don't you know that? Yes, no . . . either way, tomorrow will come. I'm just trying to tell you that I like you. That I want you. I don't believe in the whole seventeenth-century, Puritanical attitude. But if you do, well, that's all right. Maybe that's still how it's done back on the farm."

"It's not that."

"What is it then?"

She shrugged. "It's just . . ."

"What?"

"My name's not Carrie."

He nodded and touched her cheek. "I'm sorry, Dorothy."

She said nothing.

"Dorothy," he repeated, pronouncing each syllable. "On you, that is a beautiful name."

She stood, putting his card in her pocket, and crossed the room to where a party of four had entered and seated themselves. "What can I get you?" she asked them. When she turned from their table, Harold had gone.

She took a deep breath.

From within the kitchen, Nancy Bing called Dorothy's name.

Dorothy pressed through the swinging double doors that led out of the dining room.

"Well?" Nancy asked, standing at the sink washing dishes.

"They want four Darjeelings," she answered.

"Not them!" Nancy said. "Him! What happened?"

"I don't know for sure."

"He's got eyes like Valentino," Nancy said.

That night, Dorothy stood for almost thirty minutes on the dark sidewalk outside Harold's building. She watched his window four floors above. Sometimes she saw his shadow moving across the ceiling, pacing. Was he working? she wondered. Was he struggling to find just the right word for an insightful new article on Cubism? Or was he painting—his crazy lines (abstract as the alphabet) somehow coming together to make a picture of strange power, a "Harold Burke." Or—most intriguing of all—was he pacing his floor in anticipation of Dorothy's arrival? But then she had never actually agreed to come to him, she thought; how then could he be impatient for her when even she had not yet decided whether she would knock at his door at all?

Except, of course, she had decided.

Climbing the stairs in his building, Dorothy removed from her bag the small drawing that Nancy Bing had given her to show to Harold.

Dorothy was happy to bring her friend's drawing; after all, she shared Nancy's hope that Harold might mention the work in *The Broom* or *The Dial*; also, Dorothy had been taught never to call at someone's home without an offering of some sort (problematic in this case as neither flowers nor bootleg whiskey seemed appropriate); finally, she hoped the drawing would divert attention from her nervousness in the first moments after Harold opened his door. Wouldn't an *objet d'art* provide something to talk about if conversation flagged? When Dorothy reached the fourth floor, mere steps from Harold's apartment, she glanced to see which of Nancy's drawings she had sent along.

It was a reclining nude. "Oh, great . . ." Dorothy muttered.

She knocked at the door.

Harold answered, inviting her in.

I'm modern, I'm modern, she thought. Harold's apartment was just as she imagined it.

"I'm glad you've come."

Harold took the drawing from Dorothy's hand, glanced at it, then set it on a table beside the bed.

"That's a gift for you," Dorothy said.

"Oh, thank you."

"Well, it's not actually from me."

"Who's it from?"

"My friend Nancy Bing. You know, at the Proper Pagan. The other waitress."

"Oh, right."

"She's an artist."

"Oh," he answered. He had not taken his eyes from Dorothy since she stepped into the room.

She looked away.

"There's no need to be shy," he said.

She laughed.

"You and me, Dorothy. We're old pals now."

"Oh yeah?" she asked. "One whole day?"

"One whole day and night."

"Oh."

"Would you like a drink?"

"No."

"Sit down."

"All right." She sat on the chair beside the desk.

He sat nearby on the bed. "Now, tell me who you are, Dorothy."

"Hmmm, that's not an easy question. Where do I begin?" What was she going to tell him? That as a girl she'd been swept away by a tornado to a magical, far-away land peopled by witches and wizards and talking animals? No one had ever believed that—no matter how much she insisted to friends and family that it was true. They all believed she had been concussed by the storm. Or, worse, that she possessed a touch of madness. So, years before, she had set the entire fantastical episode from her mind until now she almost believed that it *had* been nothing more than a mere dream. Or that she *had* been concussed. Or that she was a touch mad. "I don't know where to begin," she said.

"At the beginning."

She said nothing.

"That's all right, Dorothy. Maybe instead of telling me who you are you can show me."

Show him? Wasn't she right here, before him now? What more was there to show of herself? Except, of course, the rest of her, the still-hidden parts. True, she felt safe with Harold Burke—familiar. Nonetheless, he had said very little about himself. Why? What was *his* story? Was now the time to ask? She did not know the proper etiquette for these circumstances. Farm girls from Kansas were not trained for this. But then perhaps this was her training, she thought. Here, now. All of this: a mere exercise. Except . . . if this moment alone with Harold Burke was not the object of all she had already learned but was merely another lesson, then what might lay beyond? Love? Was that the final, real thing? The true object of experience? Dorothy knew she did not love Harold. At least, not yet. She took a deep breath. She did not want to think about any of these things any longer. She tried to stop thinking (which she feared she did far too much anyway). She chose to trust Harold. She would let him guide her through the night. He had asked her to tell him who she was—she hadn't the words. But now he was asking her to show him who she was. Perhaps that would go better.

She stood from the chair and went to where he sat on the bed.

She bent until their faces were inches apart.

He smiled and slipped one hand around the back of her neck, urging her closer. He ran his mouth from the base of her chin, up the tender skin along the line of her jaw and whispered her name into her ear. His breath was warm. Necking, she thought. All the rage. "Dorothy, Dorothy . . ." he said. He seemed to know what he was doing.

They kissed.

Hours later, asleep in Harold's bed, Dorothy dreamed of being back in her aunt and uncle's house as it was lifted off the ground in a great, swirling storm—in the dream she raced from bedroom to bedroom, but could find no one home.

"Auntie Em?" she cried, sitting up in the bed.

She opened her eyes. It was morning.

She was tangled in Harold's sheets.

"Harold?"

The whole night rushed back to her. "My God . . ." she thought.

Harold turned to her from across the room, where he had been bent over the desk, looking at Nancy's drawing. He was already shaved and dressed. "How are you this morning, Dorothy?"

"Good, I think." She pulled the bed sheets around her. "And you?"

He said nothing, but turned back to the drawing.

"Do you like it?" she asked.

"No," he answered, tapping his finger on the paper. "Your friend has no technique at all. I mean, drawing's not just about scattering lines on a page. Modernism is not mere foolishness." He showed her Nancy's drawing. It did not look as good to Dorothy in the morning light as it had looked the night before. "What is the intention?" he continued. "I mean, what's your friend trying to do, Dorothy?"

"I don't know, exactly," she answered. Harold, the blistering art critic. This was not what she had expected him to be like with her in the morning.

"Well, whatever she's after, she's missed it," he said.

"I'm sorry to hear that."

"But you . . ." he said.

"What about me?"

He turned the drawing over. "Did you write this?"

"On the back?"

He nodded.

"It's just a note," she answered. "Why? Is something wrong with it?"

He shook his head no. A smile spread across his face. "You're a goddamn poet, Dorothy."

"What?"

"Why didn't you tell me?"

"What are you talking about?"

"I mean, it doesn't look like a poem, but if you break up the lines just right and play with the punctuation a little and cut a few words . . ." He took a pencil from the desk and then crossed the room to sit beside Dorothy on the bed.

"Are you making fun of me?"

"Of course not. Look." He copied her own note, but scattered the words in a new way on the back of the drawing.

She watched. Now, her words read as follows:

Nancy drew
this picture
with color (pencils)

won from
a carnival (barker)
even as she
missed the bull's-
eye again

and again
and.

"Do you see?" he asked.

"Well, it is something. But a poem?"

He kissed her. "It's good, Dorothy. I'm not a literary critic, I'm an art critic, but I know what I like."

"Yeah?"

"Sure. I like you, for example." He kissed her again. "And I like your poem too. And, believe me, I know they're two separate things. It's not your soft skin I'm commenting on here. It's your words. They're so alive. Of course, that's not to say I don't like your skin too."

She looked at the poem. "It doesn't have a title," she observed.

"Well, most modernist poems don't."

"Then how do you tell them apart?"

"Sometimes they're numbered," he answered. "Other times they're known by their first line."

"Hmmm. 'Number One'?" she said.

He nodded.

"I'm a poet?" she laughed. Dorothy had secretly written poems from the time she was a small girl. However, they had been rhymed and syrupy—now, she was glad she had never shown them to anyone. She understood that they had been hopelessly nineteenth century. But this! It seemed so simple. And modern. She liked the way the poem looked on the page. She knew it would not be difficult to learn to re-arrange words like this herself. She liked modernity a lot.

He gave her the pencil. "Go ahead and sign it," he said.

She signed her name. Dorothy Gale.

"You're my one and only," he said, kissing her.

However, she was not his one and only.

Three weeks after their first night together, Harold Burke moved away from New York with a wealthy widow who owned a mansion near Atlanta, Georgia. He explained to friends around the Village that it was the widow's southern accent that he had been unable to resist. He did not say goodbye to Dorothy, who had continued visiting him every few nights (unaware of his southern belle) right up to the night before he left New York. After he was gone, Nancy Bing consoled Dorothy by clarifying precisely what Harold Burke was and was not; that is, he *was* an ass (not to mention an incompetent art critic in Nancy's opinion) and he was *not* the only man on Earth. However, Dorothy did not need reminding of these things. Nor did she need consoling. She did not think she missed him. She was too busy writing poetry to miss Harold Burke or any man, though she suspected that when she wrote her memoirs he would occupy a prominent place—one that acknowledged him for his inspiration and forgave him for his weaknesses, which Dorothy addressed in detail in fourteen of the first fifteen modernist poems she wrote the first week after his departure (the best of which was an ode called, "Oh, Har-old-old-old"). Nonetheless, none of these new poems seemed to capture the vitality of her first, which caused Dorothy the poet great consternation . . .

❖

Rita Gaspereaux closed the book and rested her head on the desk, drifting to sleep. In a dream, she was returned to the mortuary chapel, where that day Cletus Gaspereaux had lain in a closed coffin. Now, as then, Rita sat alone in the first row on a pine bench; organ music played on a Victrola. Blaisedale sat with eyes closed in silent meditation beside the coffin. Someone tapped Rita's shoulder from the row behind. She turned. The tall, thin detective named Hammett doffed his hat to her. His eyes were kind, but the lines around his mouth suggested a capacity for cruelty. She liked that. She'd go with him any time.

"You're alone now," he observed.

"No, there's still you."

He looked away.

"I remember you," she said. "You walked me around the hotel suite. I was incapacitated, but you were kind. You're a gentleman. Unlike the rest of those bastards."

Hammett shook his head. "I'm no gentleman."

"Well, there's still the Falcon," she said.

"Yeah. Whatever the hell it really is."

"You don't know?"

"I know it's worth a fortune. Same as everybody else knows."

"Why are you here?" she asked.

"To pay my respects, of course."

"You're lying, Mr. Hammett."

Whereupon the dream ended and the next thing Rita knew she was awake and it was morning.

She sat up at the desk, forgetting the dream.

Her arms ached from having supported her head on the desktop all night. Asleep, she had knocked *Dorothy G., Kansas* onto the floor. She should have moved herself into the bedroom. But no one had awakened her to say it was time to leave her book behind. Her father, Moira, Floyd, Wilbur, Emil—gone. Bastards all of them, she thought, rubbing her eyes.

They could go to Hell.

She had never chosen to live as they lived. One hotel after another. The money, the lies, the strange men. Just a few weeks before, aboard ship in the South China Sea, she had voiced her dissatisfaction to Gaspereaux (though he was not a man with whom one could ever hope to win an argument). "I didn't choose to be brought into this world," she told him.

He had smiled and opened his fat palms as if in supplication. "I like a daughter who feels free to complain about her life, even to the most devoted and generous of fathers." His English accent and manner was well studied—no gentleman, perhaps, but a butler in a fine house . . . "I don't trust a girl who lacks gumption, spunk," he continued, taking a sip from a silver-plated hip flask. "Passivity makes a girl unreliable. I congratulate you for your 'fighting spirit,' my dear. It will serve you well in the years ahead. Nonetheless, I can't believe you would prefer living as a boring, cow-eyed farm girl or a thin-lipped, cold-blooded blue-stocking to living as the exciting cosmopolitan you are. Why, you're a spectacular example of sophisticated girlhood, my dear."

"I don't feel like it," she said.

"You're in touch with your feelings," he replied. "That's good. I don't trust a girl who isn't. If one doesn't know what one feels, how can one express oneself truthfully? But feelings are not facts, my dear. Let me remind you that just last month I directed Moira to take you to an opium den. I do not think I am incorrect in recalling that you liked it."

"No, you're not incorrect."

"Few girls your age have had experiences like that. Nonetheless, I like a girl who yearns for more, always more. I know you well, Rita. That's why I'll see to it that you'll never live as some sort of anemic prude. No, my dear, the world is your oyster. And I continue to delight in introducing you to many interesting and accomplished men and women, some of them twice and three times your age, who are only too glad to share their worldliness with you."

That he did.

"But in order to continue being a true sophisticate," he concluded, "you will have to tolerate the life that I have chosen for you."

Now, Rita stood from the desk, stretching her limbs. True sophisticate, my ass, she thought. She had learned from Gaspereaux the names of a few fine wines and how to discern the difference between local hooch and fine Tennessee sipping whiskey (no mean trick in an era of Prohibition). But there was much she did not know. He had made all arrangements for their travel; he paid all bills, ordered all meals, and determined in some fashion he never shared who would serve as the next mark in whatever con game they played to raise their capital, which he invested . . . somewhere. And, more specifically, there were "ordinary" aspects of a girl's life that she had not mastered, which she suspected came as second nature to other girls. For example, friendship. She had read stories in which friendship proved valuable in one way or another to the success of a heroine. The first and most important of such stories was *The Wonderful Wizard of Oz*. Perhaps that was why Rita was enjoying *Dorothy G., Kansas* so much. Years before, her father had pointed out that in the Oz story little Dorothy had no child-aged friends, but happily made do with adult friends. For a long time thereafter, Rita tried to identify the members of her own company with Dorothy's companions. Wilbur Clark as the Scarecrow, Floyd Bradley as the Tin Man, Emil Madrid as the Cowardly Lion, Moira O'Shea as Glinda the Good Witch (or sometimes the Wicked Witch), and her father as the all-powerful wizard. It never felt right. And there were other books, other examples of girls aided by friendship. But Rita never had any friends, and though she eventually came to believe that friendship was a mere literary invention—as inorganic as iambic pentameter, but useful to an author as a means of concealing the darkest truths about human relations from brain-addled readers—she also suspected she'd be better able to manipulate its appearance if she had been allowed to experience a bit of it as a child.

She stood from the desk, stretching her limbs, and moved from the desk toward the master bedroom, into which she had not gone the previous night. The following facts seemed to her manifest: Emil was lying about her mysterious parentage; Mr. DeMille or Mr. Von Stroheim or Mr. Griffiths was going to love her almost as a daughter; now was no time to go soft.

She opened the door of the master bedroom.

A man's obese body lay naked, face up on the bed. It was no living thing.

At first, she thought it a hallucination.

When she realized it was real, she gasped and turned from the bedroom. She stumbled back into the sitting room and made her way to the window that overlooked Geary, pressing her face against the glass until it fogged. After a moment, she gathered herself and slowly made her way back to the doorway.

She peered in. "Father?"

The head was wrapped in thick gauze and rested like a puff of cotton atop the fat neck; the face had been too mangled by gunshot for the damnable undertaker to attempt repair. The hands were crossed in repose upon the massive, sagging belly. The pallid skin was a moldy blue-green in places; the shriveled penis was a mere bud among hardened mounds of fat. She looked again at the cotton-enshrouded head. It had to be her father's corpse, hadn't it? Without seeing the face, she couldn't be sure. Wouldn't it be like him to have staged his own murder to avoid criminal prosecution? Or was that mere paranoia speaking? All she had to do was approach the corpse and unwind the cotton concealing the head to know for sure. So, she gathered herself and stepped into the room, which smelled of formaldehyde and worse.

As she moved to the bed, bile rose in her throat. She fought it down and then reached for the cotton wrapping.

She stopped.

It *had* to be her father's body. She didn't need to see whatever was left of the face. That was asking too much, even of her. Besides, the issue was not who the body belonged to (of course it was Cletus Gaspereaux) but why it was here. She turned away, and on a bedside night table she found a typed note that seemed to answer the question:

Dear Miss Gaspereaux,

In the interest of fair business practice, we must insist that the cash fees you paid yesterday ($140) as well as the clothing and jewelry you supplied for the burial of your father, Cletus Gaspereaux Esq., be applied to your fraudulent transaction with us of last year, wherein we at Blaisedale & Son were left with an abandoned, unidentifiable body and defrauded of a $220 unsecured loan made to you at that time. The herewith returned remains of Cletus Gaspereaux have been prepared for burial, including embalming, for which an additional fee of $45 has been assessed. Further fees of $15 for this afternoon's use of our chapel and $5 for the transport of the body from our establishment to your hotel, balance our transaction and bring our professional relationship to a conclusion. The city is full of other outstanding mortuaries, any one of which we are sure will be happy to complete the internment/memorial process, provided you pay cash.

I know you will treat this matter with extreme discretion, as any adverse publicity will surely bring your history of fraud to the attention of the authorities.

With sympathies for your loss,
Mrs. Lorraine Blaisedale

The wife?

Rita could not be sure if the signature was authentic. But it didn't matter. Either way, the letter indicated that the undertaker had overcome his trepidation. She wadded the note and tossed it across the room. "Tom Mix my ass," she muttered. She went to the closet, from which she removed her suitcase, averting her eyes from the stinking mound of flesh on the sagging mattress; next, she went to the chiffonier, from which she removed her clothes, tossing undergarments into a bag.

The corpse could rot for all she cared. She had been a sentimental fool ever to have thought otherwise. When she finished packing her two bags, she carried them out of the bedroom and into the sitting room, slamming the door between the rooms.

She sat in a chair, her heart pounding.

She noticed she had broken a fingernail. "Goddamn!" she said.

Her train left at 10:24. The ticket would cost $7.40, leaving her with just over fifty dollars.

Of course, there were ways of raising more money, but . . .

She gathered herself and went to the desk where she had slept through the night. There, she picked up her pen and the hotel notepad and scribbled the following note:

> *To whom it may concern: Do what you will with the refuse you find in this room. Your furnace will likely serve as well as any crematorium. And, while burning a corpse is unpleasant, please be assured that this man's soul is already long departed, burning even now elsewhere.*

She put down the pen and turned toward the window. Below, the street was crowded with traffic. She looked to the horizon, where the hills of Marin County were a pale shade of green, their color diffused by wisps of fog that hovered over the bay. Was she looking south toward Hollywood? Or was she looking in the opposite direction?

Her sense of direction was never good.

"Miss Gaspereaux?" a woman's voice inquired from behind her.

Rita jumped and turned at the sound, expecting a chambermaid. Instead, a young woman she did not recognize stepped in from the hall through the opening double doors of the suite.

"Who are you?" Rita demanded. "Who invited you in?"

"I knocked," the woman said. "But there was no answer."

"How dare you just walk in?"

"I'm sorry," the woman said. "But I heard you speaking and you sounded distressed and since the door was unlocked I thought I'd best check on you."

"I wasn't speaking to anyone," Rita snapped. Had she been reading the note aloud as she wrote it? "No one else is here." She glanced at the closed door that led to the master suite, where her father's corpse lay. "How could you have heard me speaking? I'm alone. And I didn't invite you in. Now get out!"

The woman turned as if to go, then she stopped. "You are Rita Gaspereaux, aren't you?"

Rita nodded.

"My name is Evie LeFabre," the woman continued.

Rita glanced again at the bedroom door, then forced her attention away from it. "What do you want?"

"May we speak a moment?"

"About what?"

"The Black Falcon."

"Are you a reporter?"

"No."

Rita sized her up: she was a few years older, perhaps twenty-two—lanky, brown-haired, athletic; her attire was modest and freshly pressed; while not unattractive, Miss LeFabre lacked the pizzazz to move a big spender across a dance floor or to capture the generous affections of a dying, octogenarian millionaire or to dissuade a police captain from doing his job by the mere flutter of her eyes (all of which Rita had accomplished more than once). Rather, she seemed better suited to typing documents in an insurance agency or marrying a clerk and retiring to motherhood, Rita thought. Assignations in a hotel as luxurious as this with a young woman as wily as Rita would seem to strain her capacities.

"You don't work for the police, do you?" Rita asked.

Evie smiled. "Heavens, no."

"Then get the hell out of my room."

"But it's of the utmost importance."

Rita gathered herself. "Leave your name at the front desk, Miss LeFabre." That was how it was done, wasn't it? "Perhaps I'll contact you later. But now, leave my room."

"But I have sensitive information for you."

"About what?"

The LeFabre woman glanced at the closed bedroom door. "Are we alone?"

Rita was not sure how to answer. Might the undertaker have alerted the hotel to the presence of the corpse? Was this a setup? "No one's listening to us," Rita answered. "If that's what you mean."

"Good."

"I'll talk to you downstairs, in the lobby," Rita suggested.

"No, that's impossible," Miss LeFabre answered. "We might be eavesdropped upon."

"Look, what do you want? Can't you see I've packed my bags and I'm on my way out?"

"Glad I caught you."

"Caught me?"

"I have something to share with you."

"What?"

"I don't mean to be forward, Miss Gaspereaux, but wouldn't it be polite to ask me to sit down?"

"Yes, it would be polite. *If* I had invited you in."

Evie LeFabre said nothing.

Rita pointed to one of the Queen Anne chairs bedside the tea cart in an alcove of the suite.

"Thank you." Miss LeFabre sat. "You must forgive my nervousness. I've never done anything like this."

"Who are you?"

"I work as a secretary for the Pinkerton Detective Agency. I'm assigned to two operatives who sometimes work as partners. Mike Arnette and Sam Hammett."

Rita betrayed nothing on her face.

"Mr. Hammett visited you a few days ago," the secretary said.

Rita remained silent.

"I believe he came to this very suite," Evie continued. "Perhaps you don't remember. I understand you'd been drugged."

"Look, what's this all about?"

"The Falcon."

"It was a fake. I already know about it."

"No you don't. No one does, but me."

"Miss LeFabre, I have a train to catch."

"Have you seen today's paper?"

"No."

Evie handed Rita a clipping. "Read it, please."

Murder of Sea Captain Linked to Black Falcon Affair

San Francisco, CA—Police confirm a link between last week's murder of Louis Doyle, Master of the thirty-ton freighter *La Paloma*, and the recent criminal activity known as the Black Falcon Affair. "Captain Doyle was shot multiple times by Wilbur Clark, bodyguard of racketeer Cletus Gaspereaux, in an unsuccessful attempt to take from the Captain's possession the small sculpture known as the Black Falcon," said Tom Paulsen of the San Francisco Police Department at a press conference in the Hall of Justice this afternoon. "It is believed that Doyle had transported the *objet d'art* aboard his ship from Hong Kong in partnership with Moira O'Shea, who was later arrested in connection with the recent criminal spree."

Doyle's shooting occurred on the night of the 26th at Miss O'Shea's apartment, located on the one thousand block of California Street. A man of great physical strength, Captain Doyle managed, despite his wounds, to escape his assailants and make his way to the Pinkerton Detective Agency, where he died immediately after delivering the Black Falcon into the hands of a private investigator whose name is being withheld by police pending further investigation.

Wilbur Clark was later slain in a shootout with S.F.P.D. after he gunned down his employer, racketeer Cletus Gaspereaux, on Post Street.

"The irony of the whole affair," Paulsen said, "is that the statuette is a counterfeit. Nonetheless, the results of its violent pursuit, which continue to reveal themselves to our shocked, law-abiding city, are sadly authentic."

"'Shocked, law-abiding city'?" Rita asked. "Isn't that piling it on a bit thick?"

"Well, it is shocking," Evie said.

"Is that what you came here to say?"

Evie lowered her voice and drew nearer. "I came to tell you that there is an inaccuracy in the newspaper article."

"It wouldn't be the first time, Miss LeFabre."

Evie folded the clipping and placed it in her handbag. "That's true, but no one knows about this particular inaccuracy, except me."

"Congratulations."

"Captain Doyle did not die immediately after delivering the Falcon," Evie said. "Even Sam doesn't know."

"Sam, the detective?"

"Yes, Mr. Hammett. Sam. He and I were alone in the office when

Captain Doyle staggered in. The poor man dropped a heavy package to the floor and then crumpled unconscious onto a sofa. Sam opened the Captain's overcoat and saw the blood and the holes in his chest. The police say he was shot five times. It was terrible. So, quite naturally, Sam assumed he was dead and turned his attention to the package. We unwrapped it. As you know, it was the Falcon. Well, a counterfeit. But at the time we didn't know it was a fake. And then, in a flash, Sam was out the door with the bird, gone to meet with your father and the others. He told me to call the police. But before I could dial the phone, Captain Doyle regained consciousness. Just for a moment. I was terrified."

"Why are you telling me this? I'm not involved in this Falcon affair."

"So you say," Evie answered. "And I choose to believe you."

"I'm not interested in what you 'choose,' Miss LeFabre," Rita said. "What matters is that I'm not involved. Never was. Understand? Ask the police. They believe me. And as long as there's room in the women's penitentiary for one more, it's important they continue to believe me."

"I understand your position, Miss Gaspereaux."

"I have a train to catch."

"Captain Doyle regained consciousness for only a minute before he died," Evie continued. "Actually, it was just a few seconds. But that was long enough for him to whisper to me a name and a city, which I presume is where I can find the 'real' Falcon. The priceless one."

Count Keransky, Rita thought. Well, so what? Rita wasn't interested in the damned bird. Or the damned Russian. So what did she care if this Evie knew where to find him? In any case, she knew better than to ask outright where he was. Nobody ever got straight answers doing that. "Why would the dying Captain share this 'valuable' information with you?"

"I don't think he knew who he was talking to. He was shot full of holes. It was horrible, Miss Gaspereaux. I've never seen anything like it. Have you ever seen a dead body?"

Rita thought of the corpse in the next room. "Yes, I have."

"Oh, I still shudder to think about poor Captain Doyle. The police marvel that he walked all the way from Miss O'Shea's apartment to our office, as shot up as he was. You must understand, he was not a big man but his strength was almost superhuman, which leads me to believe that he wanted very badly to deliver his message."

"Well, aren't you fortunate to have been there to hear it?"

"I've come to share it with you," Evie continued.

"Why would you do that?"

"I've tried to keep it to myself. But it's too much for me to contain."

"Maybe you should tell your boss, Hammett."

"He wouldn't be interested anymore."

"Why not?"

"He's getting out of the detective business," Evie answered. "It never agreed with his health."

"Being a gumshoe doesn't agree with anybody's health."

"No, but he's got real bad lungs. See, he contracted tuberculosis in the Great War."

Rita didn't give a damn.

"So now he's going to start writing mystery stories," Evie continued. "Oh, he's talked about doing it for a long time, but he never got around to it. Until now. Since the Falcon case wrapped up. You should hear his typewriter clattering away. He finished two or three stories in just the past week and is going to mail them off to magazines. He signs the stories, 'Dashiell Hammett.' I mention it just in case you're ever browsing through one of the pulps and happen to see one."

Rita didn't read the pulps. "I thought you said his name was Sam. What kind of name is Dashiell?"

"It's his middle name."

"Oh."

"But I wouldn't tell him what I know about the Falcon, even if he was still interested," Evie said.

"Why not?"

"He's not the man I thought he was."

Rita remembered him. Tall, handsome.

"Did you know he turned Moira O'Shea over to the police?" Evie asked.

"Yes, I know."

"And you know what she did to herself in prison a couple of days ago?"

Rita nodded. "How does this relate to your boss?"

"Sam loved her," Evie answered. "I saw the two of them together. Sure, she was crooked. But Sam's no angel. He was always willing to do whatever it took to complete a case, believe me. He's broken laws. Broken heads once in a while too. You can't imagine some of the stuff he did for the Pinkertons up in Montana. But I always thought his heart was good. So who's to say Moira's heart couldn't have been good too, despite the things she's done?"

Evie LeFabre could not be more wrong about a woman, Rita thought.

"Now, I'm not saying he should have gone off and married her," Evie continued. "No, they didn't belong together in that permanent sort of way. Still, I saw how they looked at each other. But this Falcon business . . . I always knew Sam could be hard-hearted when it came to cases. But turning Moira over to the police . . . I wouldn't have believed he was capable of that. And then when she attempted to take her own life . . ."

"Attempted?" Had Emil lied to her?

"Yes, she was cut down by guards, just in time. She survived."

Indestructible bitch, Rita thought.

"But she won't be coming back into Sam's life any time soon," Evie continued. "Not with the years of imprisonment she's facing."

"What's it to you?"

Evie said nothing.

Suddenly, Rita understood. "Ah, I see. You love him."

"No."

Rita said nothing.

"Okay, once I did, maybe," Evie admitted. "But what I used to feel for him doesn't matter anymore. I've quit my job."

"Why haven't you gone to the police?"

"The Falcon is priceless," she answered.

"And you want to get it?"

Evie nodded.

"Money means a great deal to you?" Rita asked.

"No more than to most."

"Then it means a great deal."

"But it's not the money."

"What is it?"

"Sam used to tell me that someday I'd make a good detective. But he never meant it. He never saw me that way—clever, cunning. The truth is he never saw me at all."

Rita moved to the double doors, opening one to indicate it was time for her uninvited guest to leave. "I'm not interested in your sappy motives, understand? If you want the statuette and you know where it is, go get it. I don't care one way or the other."

"I'll share the profits with you."

Rita shook her head no.

"The truth is," Evie continued, "Sam's right. I'm not clever enough. I'm not cunning. I can't manage it alone. But you . . . well, please take no offense, but you've been raised among thieves, Miss Gaspereaux, which is all to your advantage. I need your help."

"Goodbye, Miss LeFabre. I have an appointment with Hollywood. I'm going there to become a motion picture actress."

"Oh, I love the movies."

"Good for you."

"Who's your appointment with? Maybe I'd recognize the name."

"No one specifically."

"But you said . . ."

"I meant I had an appointment with Hollywood in general. You know, metaphorically."

Evie looked confused. "So one day I may see your picture in the fan magazines?"

"That's quite likely."

"How exciting!"

"Yes, I should be on my way now."

"But surely you're not abandoning your search for the Black Falcon."

"I told you, I'm not involved."

"But they're all gone now."

"Who?"

"The ones who've been looking for it."

"That damned bird destroyed them all, Miss LeFabre. Why would I pursue the same fate?"

"Failing to find the bird is what destroyed them, Miss Gasperaux."

Now she was sounding like Emil, Rita thought. Might they be in this together? No matter, she'd had enough. "Even if I wanted to go after the bird, which I don't, why would I go with you?"

"Because I know where to look for it."

"Suppose I told you I already have a pretty good idea of its location." She didn't, of course.

"Maybe you do," Evie answered. "But time is of the essence, and from what I read in Sam's case notes, you don't have enough money to make the necessary voyage."

"What does your boss know about my finances?"

"He searched your suite before the police got to it."

"What?"

"Yes, while you were being questioned at the station. Oh, don't worry, he didn't steal anything. He never would. Strange, isn't it, how a man can be so upright and trustworthy in some ways and yet such a cad in others? But according to his calculations you only have a few hundred dollars."

If only she had that much left . . . "What does my money have to do with any of this?"

"I've been to my bank," Evie said.

Rita closed the door of the suite, stepping toward Evie.

"I've withdrawn my entire savings to cover our expenses." From her handbag, Evie removed a stack of bills, which she waved about. "Almost four and a half thousand dollars."

"What, exactly, are you proposing, Miss LeFabre?"

"I'm proposing that you and I take a little trip," she said, returning the cash to her handbag. "To retrieve the Falcon."

"Retrieve? That makes it sound like it once belonged to us."

"You're right," Evie said. "I mustn't be a coward. I'll say it like it is. I'm asking you to help me steal the Falcon and then split the profit, fifty-fifty. I'm new to the game, but I have very specific information. And I have resources. And I'm prepared to do whatever is necessary to get the Falcon."

Rita said nothing.

"You must believe me, Miss Gaspereaux. I've been law-abiding all my life, but that's over now. What did it ever get me?"

Rita wanted to be rid of the secretary, but the forty-five hundred in the handbag prevented her. She drew nearer, like a confidant: "Honesty among thieves is no mere cliché, you know," she said. "Not if partners in crime are to have any success. If what you're proposing is theft, then say it outright. To me, at least."

"Then you'll work with me?"

"I didn't say that."

"But you used the word 'partners.'"

Had this woman's experience working around private dicks (one of whom she girlishly perceived as a knight in shining armor) taught her nothing? Next thing, Rita thought, the woman would prick her finger and suggest they make a blood pact to seal their partnership as in *The Adventures of Tom Sawyer*. Of course, Cletus Gaspereaux had warned

Rita about pigeons whose naïveté seemed too good to be true. But he had also taught her that one must move through the world with hungry eyes always open. And a bankroll never hurt an aspiring motion picture actress, especially one who was otherwise broke. "Are you truly prepared to embark on a life of crime?" Rita asked, as melodramatically as possible.

"Whatever is necessary," Evie answered.

Rita surmised it would not be difficult to get the forty-five hundred out of the secretary's handbag and into her own. A night or two traveling together . . . She could easily make it appear the theft had been engineered by someone else, as she had no desire to be badgered afterward by either Evie LeFabre or the police. "Where would we have to go to retrieve this Falcon?" she asked, as if it mattered to her.

"You mean you don't know where it is?"

Rita shook her head no.

"Europe."

"Can you be a bit more specific?" she asked. "Europe's a pretty big place."

"I'm afraid I can tell you no more than that."

"You don't trust me?"

"I shouldn't, should I?"

"Only to a point, I suppose." She almost felt sorry for the secretary. But then, mightn't taking her forty-five hundred actually be doing her a favor by preventing her from entering a "life of crime," which can be lethal for those unsuited to it? Busted flat, the secretary would return to the security of an insurance office or accounting firm—where she belonged. Eventually, she might recall the experience as an expensive but instructive adventure, something of interest to tell the grandchildren—perhaps the only thing of interest (not that such a justification was necessary in the case of an opportunity as ripe as this, Rita thought). "In time, Miss LeFabre, I suspect we'll come to understand one another like old friends."

"Yes, I think so."

Rita sat in the chair beside Evie. "Why don't you let me hold the cash?" she suggested.

Evie did not move. After a moment: "No, Miss Gaspereaux. That's not a good idea."

"Very good. I was testing you. You're going to do all right."

"Then you're in?" Evie asked.

Rita nodded.

Evie smiled, then grew sober as she leaned across the tea cart to take Rita's hand. "Oh, I've been so anxious about this proposition that I've been very rude."

"How's that?"

"Your father," Evie continued. "I neglected to express my sympathies, which I can assure you are heartfelt and sincere. You see, I lost my father a few years back and I know how grieved you must be."

"Yes, grieved."

"I understand the service was yesterday."

"Yes."

"I would have come to pay my respects, but I thought it best if we were not seen together by others."

"Well, aside from the mortician and your boss there were no others."

"Oh, I'm sorry. The world can be so unforgiving."

"He was not a well-loved man."

Evie stood. "Yes, well. It's always painful to lose a parent, regardless of his faults."

"Believe me, nothing mattered to him beyond his own flesh and blood."

"Exactly," Evie said, touching Rita's hand. "His own flesh and blood. That's you."

"Oh, he wasn't my real father," Rita said, surprising herself with her candor. She stopped.

"You were adopted?"

"No."

"But you said . . ."

Rita cut her off. "Let's not discuss family just now."

Evie nodded and withdrew a packet of papers from her handbag. "I've booked a private compartment for the two of us to New York City. First class. The train leaves in fifty-five minutes. Beyond that, I'll say no more, though I must admit I'm quite excited by the prospect of travel. When I bought the train tickets, I felt more like a tourist than a business traveler, serious as our business is."

You are a tourist, Rita thought. You'll always be a tourist. Wherever you go. On a train, on a boat, here in San Francisco, and even in the two-bedroom walk-up you no doubt share with your widowed mother—a tourist. Yes, a tourist through life. A tourist in your own head.

"Call me Rita."

"Let me help you with your bags, Rita."

Rita nodded and turned back to the writing desk to gather up the novel, *Dorothy G., Kansas*, which she would likely finish in the coming days. And she was thinking about the forty-five hundred dollars. Perhaps by this time tomorrow or the day after . . . Hollywood could wait that long. She picked up the book. By the time she heard the bedroom door open behind her, it was already too late.

"Oh my goodness," Evie exclaimed.

Rita turned.

Evie stood in the entrance to the bedroom with her hand still on the doorknob; she stared inside, her face gone white.

"Close the door," Rita instructed.

Evie could not move.

Rita went to her.

"I thought I'd check for any forgotten luggage," Evie said, her eyes still fixed on the man's naked corpse.

"Close the door," Rita repeated.

After a moment, Evie did as she was instructed. Otherwise, she did not move. "What's in there? I mean, who?"

"What did you see?" Rita asked.

"A dead man, naked on the bed. His head wrapped in gauze and . . ."

Rita shook her head no. "Let's try it again, what did you see in there, partner?" she repeated.

Evie hesitated. "Partner?"

"Isn't that the way you want it to be, Evie?"

"I guess so."

"What did you see in there?" Rita repeated, taking Evie by the elbow and squeezing.

"Nothing?" Evie offered.

"That's right."

"Was it your father?"

Rita looked at Evie as a stern schoolteacher might look at a slow child. "Does it seem likely that I would just leave my father's body like that?" she asked. "Besides, there was a ceremony at the mortuary yesterday, remember? Your boss was there."

Evie nodded.

"No, it's just some guy who died of a heart attack last night," Rita continued.

"Here?"

"Obviously."

"You mean that fat man was in that bed with you?" Evie pressed.

Rita said nothing.

Evie looked away. "Well, shouldn't we notify somebody?" she asked.

"What's to be done for him now? I don't even know his name."

"Why did you wrap his head like that?"

"Are we children here, or what?" Rita snapped. "Leave him be."

"But the poor housemaid . . ."

"Oh, this is the sort of thing housemaids are paid for," Rita answered. "Now, don't we have a train to catch?"

Fear was evident in Evie's eyes.

"Or have you changed your mind?" Rita pressed. Now, she had to risk her angle on the forty-five hundred. "Look if this is too much for you, then it'll be best for us to part company now. Understand?"

Evie said nothing.

"I told you a life of crime was no neat trick," Rita continued.

"Yes, you did."

"Well, what'll it be?"

Evie looked at Rita. "Who am I to judge something like this?"

Rita nodded. "The Bible says 'judge not.'"

"Last night you were sad and lonely and maybe you took a little comfort with a man who probably appreciated it greatly," Evie continued. "You didn't kill him did you?"

"No, I didn't," Rita answered.

Evie looked away. "And this morning we're in a hurry to catch a train and we haven't time for formalities that would make no difference now to anybody anyway, right?"

Rita nodded. "Thatta girl."

"Then we're off?" Evie said, gathering her gumption.

"Yes, off. That's exactly what we are."

CHAPTER THREE

S anta Fe's *Denver Behemoth* steamed east from San Francisco through a pass in the Sierras. Rita Gaspereaux and Evie LeFabre had settled into their private compartment; now it was almost midnight and because they had shut out the lights they could see from their bunks the moonlit countryside passing outside their window—mysterious pine forests and, high above, rocky peaks that were splashed white where the moon reflected off the last of the season's snows. As the train clattered over a trellis bridge, Evie asked Rita if she was sleeping yet.

"No," Rita said.

She had been thinking in the dark about Gaspereaux's bloated body. She knew the hotel would not place it in the furnace, so she wondered now if it would be placed in the same paupers' field as the abandoned bodies of the half dozen or so vagrants who had passed over the years for Rita's father among a half dozen or so swindled San Francisco undertakers (including Blaisedale). She hoped so. It pleased her to imagine that if there was an afterlife, Cletus Gaspereaux would spend it among such boneyard companions—her anonymous, "John Doe" fathers— whose stories of alcoholism and back-alley dissipation would bore him for eternity. It would be just. A pitchfork wielding, fire-breathing Satan was not necessary as Cletus Gaspereaux's punishment, she thought. Foul-breathed vagrants would be quite bad enough.

"If I'm not mistaken, when we reach the end of this bridge we'll have passed from California to Nevada. Can you believe it, Rita?"

"Ah, very exciting."

"Well, it is. For me."

Rita said nothing, but turned in her bunk away from the window, closing her eyes. It was late and she had much to accomplish in the next few days. She did not regret coming (though earlier in the dining car, Evie's monologue regarding her mother's numerous medical misfortunes had taxed Rita's patience); still, she did not want to keep Hollywood waiting too long.

"How do you think things are going so far?" Evie asked.

Rita knew that Evie was asking about their presumed Black Falcon adventure; nonetheless, she answered as if the question regarded her own plan to extricate Evie's forty-five hundred from her handbag: "Oh, fine," she said. Lifting the money was never a problem; pickpocketing was the most elementary of criminal crafts. More subtle and complex was the construction of a scenario whereby Rita could escape suspicion after the theft was discovered. "In fact," she added. "I think the plan's ahead of schedule."

"Oh? How's that?"

That afternoon in the club car—after Evie had taken her leave to freshen up in the compartment—Rita had made the acquaintance of a man in his mid-thirties named Ted Bowman. He had been sitting alone, spiking his Coca-Cola from a hip pocket flask as he sneaked glances in her direction. She knew the type: self-conscious, cowardly, but hungry to make trouble for himself. A clever girl could always have her way with such a man. She caught his eye; he looked away. She crossed to his table and sat beside him.

Now, Evie pressed Rita in their darkened compartment: "What do you mean ahead of schedule?"

Rita said nothing.

"Do you mean the train?" Evie continued. "Do you mean our being almost in Nevada?"

Rita turned about once more in her bunk. "I'm referring to acquaintanceship," she answered, still thinking of Ted, who after a little prodding had offered Rita a drink from his flask, introducing himself with a formality that reminded her of Blaisedale, the undertaker (an association that sweetened the prospect of using Ted as the fall guy for her plan). He was a college professor, traveling to a conference of archaeologists or anthropologists or sociologists. The details did not interest Rita. What mattered was that when she told him she was traveling with a prim cousin named Evie who she hoped to dump somewhere around Kansas City, provided she could find a man to join her on a weekend-long adventure, his interest piqued and he touched her hand to register his assent. He was as harmless and witless as a puppy, she thought. Tomorrow, she would visit his compartment; there, she would palm one of his possessions, a cuff link or cigarette case, which could later turn up in whatever incriminating location best served her purpose. If all went as planned, she would soon be able to head back to the West Coast, forty-five hundred dollars richer. And Ted would have a lot of explaining to do to the police and to poor Evie LeFabre, who by that time would have found his cuff link where she had once stashed her life savings.

"Acquaintanceship?" Evie asked. "Whose acquaintanceship have we made?"

Rita gathered herself. "I meant us. Our acquaintanceship, Evie. You and me."

"Oh."

"I think we're getting along far better than one might expect," Rita continued. "Especially, if you consider that we've known each other for less than twenty-four hours. Don't you agree?"

"Sure."

"Okay, goodnight then."

"Goodnight," Evie said. But after a moment, "Rita?"

"Yes?"

"What did your father tell you about the Falcon?"

"Nothing."

"Ever?"

"No."

"You were never curious?"

"My father was not a man you could press for answers."

"Do you believe it's priceless?"

"Maybe very valuable. But not 'priceless.' There's nothing that can't be bought."

"Do you really believe that, Rita?"

"Sure."

"Love? Or friendship?"

"Go to sleep Evie."

"I'm not tired."

"Try to be."

"I can't," Evie said. "Every time I close my eyes I think about Captain Doyle."

"Don't. There's nothing that can be done for him now."

"I can't get his dying out of my mind. His body, right there in the room."

Rita thought of her father's bloated corpse in the Fairmont suite.

The train clattered into the night.

"I think we've reached the far side of the bridge," Evie said. "Nevada." She sat up in her bunk, ruffling the blankets and rummaging in her bag. "Will you make a toast with me?"

Rita rolled over to face her. "You have something to drink?"

"I took a bottle from Sam's desk."

"What do you want to toast, Evie? Our enterprise?"

"Actually, I was thinking we should toast our crossing into another state."

Rita sat up. "If we toast every border crossing between here and the Atlantic we'll be too drunk to find the docks when we get there."

Evie laughed, switching on the small light beside her bunk. Illuminated from within, the window now became like a mirror.

"Is that whiskey the real thing?" Rita asked, watching Evie pour from a bottle into a water tumbler.

"What do you mean?" Evie asked.

"That bottle is pre-war, good stuff."

"Why wouldn't it be real?"

"Sometimes people keep the bottle and re-fill it with local hooch."

"Well, it was in Sam's desk. I don't know."

"No matter," Rita said, taking the tumbler.

"Should we sip it, or shoot it?"

"Shoot it," Rita answered.

"To the great state of Nevada!" Evie said.

Rita shot the whiskey. "Tell me, Evie, do you like the movies?"

"Sure."

"Okay, if you had to choose to see one of three movies, the first starring an actress named Celeste Star, the second starring an actress named Camille Bloom, and the third starring an actress named Lilliana Raintree, which would you choose?"

"Is this a joke or something?"

"No."

"I've never heard of any of those actresses."

"I know, but if you had to choose anyway."

She considered. "I'd choose whichever movie also had Chaplin in it."

"No," Rita said.

"But Chaplin's my favorite."

"No, imagine that he's not in any of them," she instructed.

"Okay, then I'd choose whichever had Buster Keaton."

"Never mind, Evie." Rita chided herself for having expected anything more from her.

"Fatty Arbuckle?" Evie said.

"Let's just be quiet and go to sleep now."

"What, you don't like comedies?"

Rita said nothing.

After a moment, Evie laughed and said: "Okay, I'd choose the Lilliana Raintree movie."

Figures, Rita thought. This week, that name was her least favorite. "Thank you."

"Sure thing."

Rita reached for her book, *Dorothy G., Kansas*, and turned on the small reading light in her berth. "If you'll excuse me now," she started.

"You're not going to sleep?" Evie asked.

"No, I'm going to read."

"What are you reading?"

"It's a novel."

"Does it have a heroine?"

"Yes."

"And a hero?"

"Of course." Rita opened the book. "We've just met him here in chapter three. So we'll see how he turns out. But I think he's going to be Dorothy's love interest."

"Will you read a little of it to me? The part about the hero?"

Rita considered. Why not? At least it would keep Evie quiet.

❖

Twenty-three-year-old Paul Darnell sat alone at a round table barely larger than a Chinese checkers board. He drank from a glass of Pernod. All but one other table on the sidewalk outside the Café Victor Hugo was unoccupied. Strasbourg, France, was quiet at mid-afternoon. At the other table, an old, mustachioed man sipped café noir while his beagle dozed, its snout resting on its master's blue espadrilles. The old man had been gazing now for almost ten minutes across the narrow cobblestone street toward a tobacco shop. Paul wondered what he saw. Perhaps he studied the tobacconist's outline, moving in the shadowed depths of the *tabac*. Or was the old man's attention fixed on one of the newspaper headlines displayed nearer the edge of the shop? Or was the old man studying one of the colorful cardboard advertisements for soap or cigarettes or magazines that were scattered about the shop entrance like paintings in an art dealer's basement. Or did he see nothing of the tobacconist's? Paul knew that sometimes thoughts altered vision. Sometimes a man could stare for hours at a tobacco shop and see something else altogether. Before the old man arrived at the Café Victor Hugo, Paul had been doing that very thing—seeing a house, a motorcycle, a brother. He knew he might watch the old man forever and never imagine what he saw.

Paul took a sealed envelope from his jacket pocket, tapping it on the table. He had carried the letter with him since early that morning when the concierge had handed it to him on his way out of the *pensione*. At that time, Paul had been too preoccupied with the prospects of the coming hour to stop and read the letter. After all, this was the morning for which he had been preparing almost four years—that is, since his brother's death in the war. He thought about those preparations. The flying lessons that had occupied his weekends and the better part of his attention during his less-than-distinguished sophomore year at Princeton; the job bussing tables, not to pay for his tuition, but to provide passage for this trip to France when college ended (which his academic expulsion caused to occur a full year earlier than anticipated); the French language tutoring with Madame Milde in the lobby of the city library; the volumes of military history and journalistic accounts of the Great War that he had read as if they contained in code an explanation as to why all that had happened had happened, which, despite their vast, footnoted research, they did not; the broken dates with his hometown girl Callie Shaw, whose patience had seemed unending until one afternoon last spring when she ran off to marry another man. Paul had never thought of such an extended period of time (four years) as a single, indivisible block. Now, however, what once seemed discreet moments seemed to Paul mere elements of a single process—the search for his brother Joe or, rather, the preparation to begin the search. Which had brought him to today. The real beginning.

He looked at his watch.

He wished Callie Shaw were here. She had been an important part of the four year block. It had been her idea that Paul seek the guidance of a spiritualist. She had gone with him to most of the dozen séances he attended back in the States, wherein exotic men or women conjured imitations of Joe Darnell's spirit with stagecraft, sleight-of-hand, ventriloquism, flickers, and a cynicism so complete that it attempted to pass itself as compassion. More than once Paul had stormed from the exotic, dimly lit rooms of the professional spiritualists, swearing off the supernatural forever; each time, however, Callie convinced him to try it once more. "It's true that most spiritualists are charlatans," she would argue. "But all you need to do is find one who isn't a fake." He doubted her argument would hold up in his Logic seminar with Professor Massey (though his attendance in class had by that time become so poor that he could not say for sure what his professor might or might not consider logical). Callie had been home with a head cold when Paul attended his last séance, which was conducted by a blind woman in Toms River, New Jersey. Despite Paul's pessimistic expectations, the séance renewed his faith in harebrained ideas. And more.

In spirits.

The medium provided no astral projections or ectoplasmic emanations. Rather, she simply demonstrated a sufficient knowledge of Joe's private life that Paul could not help but hope her supposed knowledge of his brother's afterlife was equally valid. For example, she knew that Joe used to pour icy water on Paul in the mornings to wake him for school. She knew that Joe had acquired two French postcards of naked women that he kept hidden in the bureau near the window. She knew that the last words Joe had spoken to Paul had been "See ya brother," which she claimed had been prophetic, if as yet unrealized. This news was thrilling to Paul. Callie too at first had seemed delighted. Nonetheless, she was displeased with what the medium's suggestions required of Paul.

Flying lessons, France.

That was when Callie ran off with the other guy.

❖

Evie interrupted Rita's reading. "Do you believe in the afterlife, Rita?"

Rita lowered the book. "What?"

"The afterlife."

"I don't believe in anything I can't see with my own eyes or touch with my own hands," Rita answered.

"Well, I believe."

"Why am I not surprised?" Rita asked ironically.

Evie sat up in her bunk. "I don't mean ghosts and the like. Or spirits. I'd never go to a séance like this Paul character. And I don't believe in the ordinary Heaven and Hell. But I do think there may be a moment between life and death when, well . . . anything can happen. A whole other life, for example, experienced from beginning to end in what would seem to those still here as the mere blink of an eye, as brief as someone's final breath. But to the dying person, it would seem eternal."

"A whole imagined life lived all in an instant?"

"Exactly."

"Ridiculous," Rita said.

"I wouldn't be so sure. Even Einstein said that time is an illusion. Or something like that."

"So now you're quoting Einstein?"

"Actually, the idea comes from one of Sam's stories."

"Oh, Sam." The tall detective/aspiring writer. It was too late at night to get started on him again.

"He submitted the story to all of the pulps, but none of them bought it," Evie continued.

"Gee, I wonder why," Rita answered. But sarcasm was lost on Evie.

"I think they turned it down because it was too philosophical for them," she answered. "No other reason, since it's such a compelling idea, right?"

"A whole additional life that is lived in the final moment of one's 'real' life?"

"Exactly."

"Well, it's an idea. I don't know how compelling."

"But Sam's story . . ." Evie started.

"Look Evie," Rita interrupted. "Do you want to hear more of the book or not?"

"Sure, please. Go on."

Rita picked up where she had left off.

❖❖

Neuhof Field in Strasbourg, France, had been used as a German base in the last years of the Great War. It had almost certainly been home to the massive gun that had launched the shells that killed Joe and the other pilots of the 27th Aero Squadron in their sleep. Had the artillery officer been decorated for taking out a whole squadron?

Paul had not come here for revenge.

Rather, he had come because the spiritualist said, "Your brother's spirit can still be found flying a Nieuport 17 in Alsace-Lorraine."

At first, this information had conjured in Paul's imagination a picture of his brother coursing the skies in his plane. He imagined looking into the French sky to catch a glimpse of the ghost plane, in accordance with the stories he and Joe had read together as boys about ghost ships on the bounding main. Only later did it occur to Paul that the spiritualist, who had left town shortly after he met her, might have meant that Joe's spirit could be found by one who *is flying* the French skies in a Nieuport 17.

In the three weeks since his arrival, Paul had discovered that gaining access to a working Nieuport 17 was more difficult and expensive than he had anticipated. Most of the planes used in the war had been scavenged for parts that could be adapted as spares for newer models. When at last he tracked down a working Nieuport in Alsace-Lorraine, he discovered that its owner—a pigeon-toed flyer named LeFleur—was unenthusiastic about the American's offer to rent the plane.

"Are you mad?" LeFleur asked. "You want to take my Neiuport up to look for your dead brother? Surely, my plane will not fly as high as Heaven."

Paul had made the mistake of telling the owner too much.

"No, no," he answered. "That's not it."

"Then what is *it*?"

"Um, well . . ." Paul stammered. He had been pleased to discover that LeFleur spoke English. He had thought it might give him an advantage in negotiation. But how could Paul adequately explain his intentions in any language? "I just believe that if I fly your plane in these skies it'll lead me to something important in my life . . . peace of mind, perhaps."

"Are you saying you want to commit suicide in my plane?"

"Oh, no!"

"Then what do you mean by 'peace of mind'?"

Paul had no answer. Instead, he took his American pilot's license from his pocket, handing it to the Frenchman.

"Sixty thousand francs," LeFleur said.

"What?!" Paul did the math in his head. Over a thousand dollars! He could buy a used plane for less.

"Take or leave," the owner said.

It was nearly all the money Paul had in the world. "I'll take it," he said.

Paul arrived at the airfield about seven that morning to fly the Nieuport. He carried in his jacket pocket a photograph of his brother. Joe grinning—a corny, carnival pose. The airfield was crowded with French army regulars. Pilots, mechanics, ground support. Many pilots supplemented their army pay by giving flying lessons and sightseeing excursions to discreet civilians. The Nieuport 17 sat beside one of the hangars built for the new Spad-Herbemonts. The weather was good. Paul sent the cab away; as he approached the plane, however, LeFleur raced out of the hangar. The Frenchman looked worried.

"What is it?" Paul asked.

"No flying this morning," LeFleur answered. "No, no."

"Why not?" Paul asked.

"Military inspection."

Paul looked around. "Where?"

"Not now, any minute."

"Look, we had a deal . . ."

"Besides," LeFleur interrupted. "The motor sounds bad to me."

"What?!"

"I have to repair, then test it. Are you a mechanic?"

"No, but I understand a thing or two about airplanes," Paul answered.

"Come back tomorrow."

"Look, does she fly or doesn't she?"

"Of course."

"Sixty thousand francs' worth?"

LeFleur smiled. "Truth is, *Monsieur*, most of your money's already gone back into her for repairs."

"A thousand dollars? Overnight?"

LeFleur gestured to the engine. "She has had a hard life, as you can imagine. But I am almost finished with her . . . reincarnation. All for you, *Monsieur*. Parts are not cheap. Lucky for you I am a mechanical genius. I can make one part stand for another, do you see? Besides, when you find your dead brother up there, it will seem a bargain. Come back tomorrow. Same time."

"The damn plane better fly."

"Of course, of course. I will test it myself this afternoon."

Paul returned to Strasbourg. He wandered for a long time along the banks of the river. In the old town, geraniums bloomed in a thousand window boxes. He wound his way up the cobbled streets toward the Cathedral and there climbed the 365 steps to the top of the tower to look over the ancient town. From here everything was far away. Even the ground. Everything except the sky, which was close enough to touch. He watched airplanes taking off in the distance. Eventually, he went inside and sat in the six-hundred-year-old silence.

The day passed slowly.

❖

Evie interrupted again. "Have you ever been to France? I haven't. In this book it sounds very beautiful. Ever been, Rita?"

"Why do you ask? Is that where the Falcon is?"

Evie answered too quickly, awkwardly. "No, of course that's not where it is."

She was such an amateur that Rita almost laughed.

"I was just wondering because of the book," Evie continued.

So, France it was. The Russian with his goddamned bird. Rita still didn't care. She knew what going after the thing had done to everyone who'd been in her life. She wasn't going to make the same mistake. Not for vengeance, nor fortune, nor some perverse familial curiosity—not when her future in Hollywood was likely so bright. To hell with the bird and the Russian both. But, of course, she still had to play along.

"Please go back to the book?" Evie requested, nervously.

"Sure," Rita said, smiling.

❖

Now it was late afternoon and Paul sat outside the Café Victor Hugo. The old man in the espadrilles, who sat near Paul, set a five-franc coin next to his café noir, roused his sleeping dog, and stood up. He glanced at Paul, nodding a greeting. His teeth were the color of corn. He shuffled across the street. His dog trailed behind. The two disappeared inside the tobacconist's; Paul lost sight of them. The waiter set another Pernod on Paul's table, removing the empty glass.

"*Merci*," Paul said.

The waiter disappeared.

Paul opened the envelope he had carried in his pocket all day. Inside, a letter, which read:

Dear Paul,

Your Mother and I remain confused and worried about your behavior. You are not a child. I try to keep this in mind whenever the temptation to correct or criticize you comes over me.

Nonetheless, do you have any idea how many young men would envy the opportunities you have thrown away?

Of course, it is pointless to bemoan discarded chances. We have been over all that quite enough. I cannot tolerate their further examination. Your past is past. It is your present and future that worries your Mother and me. We fear that you have chosen a subversion of life in place of the real thing. We believe that this calls for a very blunt assessment of your situation.

Paul, when your brother passed you became the sole bearer of our family's standard. One doesn't choose the circumstances of one's life. One only chooses how one reacts to them. I hate to say this, Paul, but you dishonor your brother's memory by failing to bear our standard with strength. Yes, it's a fine thing that you can fly a plane, but wouldn't it have been better to finish your degree? Yes, it's a fine thing that you're traveling in Europe, but wouldn't it be better if you were doing so to expand your resources rather than to pursue a perverse self-indulgence?

Paul, I'm going to tell you something that may be hard to hear.

Your brother would not be reduced to such aimlessness as you seem to be if it had been you and not him who had been killed. He'd have grieved over your loss, then moved on.

Finally, your mother's letters may at times seem to dilute the message I am trying to convey to you now. Do not be fooled. Your mother agrees with me, even if sometimes she too suffers from what has become a chronic weakness since Joe's death, which, by the way, is far more understandable in an aging woman than in an otherwise healthy young man.

You remain in our prayers,
Dad

❖❖

Evie interrupted again. "If my father knew where I was right now and where I was going next I'd get a letter very much like that," she observed.

Rita didn't want to talk about fathers. Anything but that. "Do you want to hear the book or not?"

"Oh, sure. Go on. Please."

❖❖

Paul folded the letter from home, returned it to its envelope, slipped it into his jacket pocket, and took a sip of his drink. He glanced across the street. From out of the tobacconist's emerged the old man's beagle, alone. In its mouth it carried a long, blue carton of cigarettes. Gauloises. Paul expected the old man to follow. He waited. No one emerged. The beagle continued down the street. Its pace—limited from the start by its short legs—was further slowed by the unwieldy cigarette carton, which the dog struggled to keep balanced in its jaws. Paul laughed. The beagle stopped, placed the carton on the cobbled street, took a few deep breaths, looked straight up into the sky as if to stretch its weary neck muscles, then picked up the carton and continued on its wobbling way. Paul glanced again into the tobacconist's. Mere shadows. Now the beagle reached the corner. It hesitated a moment, glancing in both directions. Then the dog turned right and disappeared.

Paul stood and stepped toward the narrow street, calling into the tobacconist's: "*Monsieur*?"

No answer.

"*Monsieur? Votre chien.*"

The old man emerged from the shop. He folded a fresh newspaper under one arm, squinting in the sunlight. He did not look at Paul.

"Your dog, *Monsieur*," Paul said, pointing in the direction the beagle had disappeared.

The old man ignored Paul. He turned back toward the shop. "*Au revoir*, Marcel," he called.

"*Merci*," the tobacconist answered from inside.

"*Votre chien*," Paul repeated.

The old man ignored him, moving into the street.

"*Monsieur*?" Paul called louder, fearing the old man might be deaf.

"Shhh!" the old man answered, turning to Paul. He crossed the street to the café. An arm's length from Paul, he stopped. "*Idiot*," he muttered.

"What?"

"*Oui*!" the old man said. "*Idiot*!" Without further explanation, he turned and started away in the same direction his dog had gone. Paul watched. The old man's arthritic steps were barely longer than the beagle's had been; nonetheless, the old man needed no guidance. At the first corner he turned right, tracking the beagle as accurately as any bloodhound.

Paul was alone.

Why had the old man called him an idiot? Was the old man a thief? Of course! And the beagle was his accomplice. It made sense. The old man had been "casing" the shop for some time; when the moment was right, he had crossed the street and bought a newspaper merely to distract the tobacconist from the beagle's shoplifting. Years before, Paul had read a story by E.A. Poe about an ape who was trained to murder. This trained beagle-caper was less far-fetched. By now, the old man and his dog were probably settling in an alley someplace to share an ill-gotten cigarette. Paul delighted at the prospect.

He crossed the street. "*Monsieur?*" he called as he stepped into the tobacco shop.

The tobacconist, a long-faced man, sat behind a counter crowded with cigarette lighters and penknives. A book of crosswords lay open before him.

"*Bonjour, monsieur,*" Paul said. "*Une question.*"

"*Oui?*"

"*Le vieil homme. Qu'a-t-il acheté*" What had the old man bought?

"*Pourquoi?*"

"*Curiosité,*" Paul answered. He had no intention of ratting on the old man. He merely wanted to know if his theory was correct.

"*Un journal,*" the tobacconist answered.

"A newspaper and nothing else?"

"No."

"I knew it!" Paul said aloud. He clapped his hands. Paul knew Joe would have gotten a good laugh. Then from outside, a voice:

"*Voleur!*"

Thief? Paul turned. His first thought was that the old man had been apprehended. But that was not possible. No one else had witnessed the crime—and Paul himself would never testify against a man whose beagle reminded him of Charlie Chaplin. Then, with a start, Paul realized who was being maligned.

"*L'américain!*"

The waiter from the Victor Hugo stood on the sidewalk outside the café. In his hand he waved a bill for the drinks for which Paul had forgotten to pay. "*L'addition!*" the waiter shouted, looking up and down the street, unable to see Paul in the shadows of the tobacco shop.

The tobacconist leaned toward Paul. "*Voleur?*" he whispered.

"Oh no, I'm no thief."

Paul hurried out of the shop, waving a ten-franc note at the waiter.

"Bastard!" the waiter announced as he took the money.

"Um, keep the change," Paul said.

Then, a distant explosion. As one, Paul and the waiter turned toward the sound, which seemed to have come from out of town. The tobacconist rushed out of his shop. Others poured out of the weathered buildings and into the street, looking first at one another and then in the direction from which the sound had come.

"Boom!" said a child who appeared at Paul's side.

"*Une bombe?*" the waiter said.

No bomb. A crash.

Paul turned away from the Café Victor Hugo and the *tabac*. He ran to the end of the block then darted up an alley to the main boulevard. Shopkeepers and townsfolk gathered on the sidewalk, pointing as one to the black line of smoke that rose on the horizon from the direction of the airfield.

Paul ran across the square to a cab parked near the Hotel de Ville. "Neuhof," he said, climbing into the black sedan.

By the time the cab arrived at Neuhof Field, the fire truck was pulling away from the wreckage at the end of the runway; the firemen on board the truck were silent and without expression as they passed Paul's cab, speeding in the opposite direction. The fire had consumed itself quickly. Now, as Paul jumped out of the cab and onto the dirt runway, he smelled burnt oil and canvas. His eyes teared in the acrid air. He pushed into the small crowd gathered about the wreckage. Many of them shook their heads, as if to negate the wreckage before them. "*Terminé,*" they pronounced. End. In the most important sense, it had ended even before the sound of the explosion carried the mile or so from the crash site to the Café Victor Hugo. How long does it take for an airplane to explode? Half a second? Perhaps less. Sound is slow. Death is fast. Though dozens of airplanes took off and landed each day at the airfield, Paul suspected which had been lost.

"*Monsieur* LeFleur?" he asked.

"Who?"

"*Le pilote*," Paul explained.

"Ah, LeFleur, *il est mort*," someone said. Dead.

Paul wiped at his burning eyes. LeFleur had been right that morning not to let Paul go up. But he had been wrong to go up himself this afternoon. Would it have been better if LeFleur had let Paul fly the doomed Nieuport? Surely it would have been better for LeFleur. But better too for Paul? True, there'd have been no Pernods, no beagle, no thievery, no future for Paul; but neither would there be this terrible moment when Paul came to know what those about him would never know—that his foolishness had caused this to happen. Paul forced himself to look at the wreckage, which had left a deep gash in the earth. Parts of LeFleur must now be mixed with the tussled ground, Paul thought. Just as parts of Joe had been mixed with the same French soil.

The crowd began to disperse.

The worst was this: Paul discovered himself wondering even now where he could find another Nieuport.

A voice: "Idiot," someone muttered.

Paul looked up. The old man from the café stood beside him. How had he gotten here so fast? Paul wondered. The old man smoked a Gauloises. His dog stood at his feet. The old man smiled, then reached into his jacket pocket. He extended an open pack of cigarettes to Paul.

"No."

The old man insisted.

"*Merci*," Paul said, taking a cigarette.

The old man started on his way, muttering once more: "Idiot . . ."

"No," Paul answered. "Worse."

The old man stopped, turned around, and waved away Paul's self-recrimination with his liver-spotted hand. "No, you're not *so* bad." His English was good. "Perhaps you are no pilot. But you know a thief when you see one." He smiled and indicated the cigarette and the dog. "Perhaps you are a detective?"

Then the old man and beagle were gone.

The next morning, Paul Darnell awoke in his narrow bed upstairs at the Hotel Le Roi, a forty-franc-per-night pension that had been the best accommodation he could afford even before . . .

❖

Mid-sentence, Rita stopped reading. She felt strange and put down the book.

"Something wrong?" Evie asked.

A wave of dizziness overcame Rita. She gripped the sides of her berth to keep from falling out, though the train's movement was smooth and steady. Then her heart raced; then it slowed until it seemed almost to stop.

She could not speak, but she knew from experience what had been done to her—the drink Evie had given her had been laced with some drug. She tried to imagine what, but her mind was already fogging. She watched Evie stand from her bunk and move across the dark compartment, pouring her own drink into the tiny sink. Damn her! Rita thought. She wanted to go to the secretary, grab her by the shoulders, and shake her hard enough to hurt her—as adults had shaken Rita when she was a girl. But she could no longer move. Then she could no longer remain sitting up; she slipped back onto her mattress. The ceiling above wavered and blurred. She forgot Evie LeFabre and the Black Falcon, her moldering father and even the drugged whiskey. She could think only of how tired she felt. Finally, she could not remember what had happened to make her feel this bad. For the life of her, she couldn't imagine.

Later, she awoke, feeling even worse.

Her head ached too much to move it from the pillow. Her eyelids were too heavy to open. But she heard voices. She recognized the words spoken as being English—familiar words. Nonetheless, her brain could no longer place the words in the context of a grammar or syntax (as if words and meaning were unrelated). Verbs no longer conveyed action; nouns no longer identified "things"; adjectives and adverbs no longer described. Of course, Rita knew it was her brain that was scrambled—not the words. But knowing this did not help her to discern what she was hearing. And neither did it calm the panic rising within her. So she gave herself back to the beckoning darkness, whose silence at least did not mock her.

This time, she dreamed:

In her dream she was playing poker at a round, felt-covered table in the club car of the *Denver Behemoth*. Around the table sat Gaspereaux and his associates, Emil, Moira, Floyd, and Wilbur.

"Five to stay in," the big man said to her.

She glanced at the cards in her hand. Two jacks, two queens, one king. A disorderly pile of wadded, paper money had been set before her on the table. Her stake. Five to stay in . . . She did not know what to do. What had the others been betting? How many cards had they taken? Who had been winning, who had been losing? Poker is always less about the cards in one's hand than it is about the attitude of the others at the table. Every good player knew that. Five to stay in . . . Undecided, she glanced out the window. It was daytime. Outside passed a desert crowded with cacti that stood as tall as skyscrapers; brown, snow-capped mountains marked the distant horizon. The train rattled on. Beside the tracks lay the scattered, wooden remains of a long-abandoned, weather-beaten wagon-train—dating from the first pioneer days, almost a century previous—half buried in the sand like the exposed bones of an ancient dragon.

"Well?" her father pressed.

She looked once more at her hand.

Two jacks, two queens, one king. "Hey look," she said. "It's you all!" Gleefully, she showed her hand to the others at the table, heedless of poker strategy. "Father is the king, see?" she said. "Floyd and Wilbur are the jacks. And Moira and Emil . . . two queens!" She laughed.

The others did not laugh.

"Are you in or out?" her father pressed.

"I'm in," she said, digging a five-dollar bill from her pile and tossing it into the pot. It didn't matter to Rita that she had already shown them her hand. This was no ordinary game.

Emil followed by tossing in another five spot.

"I'm in too," Floyd said; however, in place of cash, he tossed his Webley-Fosbery .38 caliber onto the pile.

"Me too," Wilbur said, tossing in his two .44s.

"Why aren't you betting with money?" Rita asked.

"They're dead," Emil answered. "Money is only for the living."

Her father placed the Falcon statuette into the pot. "I know this one is a fake," he said. "But I'm afraid it's all I have."

Rita stood from the table. "I'm out," she said. She did not want to play poker with the dead. "I need a moment alone in the observation car, if that's all right with everybody."

"Of course, my dear," Cletus Gaspereaux answered. "I like a girl who is observant."

In the observation car, Rita was surprised to discover that the train was no longer rattling through a desert but was cutting along the surface of a windswept ocean. She looked in all directions—nothing but water, white-capped. No bridge. No tracks. "This is a fine train indeed," she thought.

She rushed back to tell the others.

But they were gone. In their places at the table sat Evie LeFabre, the private detective Sam Hammett, and Ted Bowman, the professor.

"Good, you're back," Evie said.

"We were waiting for you," Ted added. "You can't really play poker with less than four."

Rita pointed out the window.

"It's the Atlantic Ocean," Hammett said.

"Where are the railroad tracks?" Rita continued.

The three at the table laughed.

Rita did not intend for the question to be funny.

"Are you in or out?" Evie asked her.

"In, I guess."

"Good," said Ted.

"What are the stakes?" Rita asked.

Then the dream was over.

"She's asking questions," a man's voice said. "That's a good sign."

Rita opened her eyes; the light burned.

"You'll be all right, Rita," a woman's voice said.

Rita managed to turn her head on the pillow. Evie LeFabre sat on a chair beside the bed.

"Hello Rita dear," Evie said. "We're so glad you're back."

Beside her stood Ted Bowman, who she recognized from her poker dream before remembering him from the club car.

"How are you feeling?" Evie asked her.

This was not the train compartment Rita remembered last occupying—it was no train compartment at all. Rather, the room was just large enough to contain a small settee, a chair, a tea table, and the bed upon which Rita laid. There was no clatter of rails; still, the room seemed to sway beneath her.

"What do you remember?" Evie asked her.

The daylight danced in upper corners, as if a swimming pool glittered outside. Rita looked around—moving her eyes and not her head. Expensive wood lined the walls; polished brass accoutrements glittered on the fixtures; rich upholstery of subtle brocade characterized the furnishings. A hotel? Then she noticed the windows. "They're round?"

"What?" Ted asked.

"The windows," Rita said.

"Oh, yes," he said. "Round."

"Your name is Ted," she said.

"Yes."

"Where am I?"

"This is your cabin."

Cabin? "We're in the woods?"

Ted smiled. "No."

"What are you doing here?"

"I've been concerned about you."

Rita looked from Ted to Evie and back again. "You two know each other?"

They nodded.

Was this another dream? "What's going on? Where are we?"

"Don't worry, everything's all right," Ted answered.

"What do you remember, Rita?" Evie asked.

"A poker game," she said. "I had two pair."

Evie turned to Ted. "What does she mean?"

He shook his head, uncomprehending.

Evie turned back to Rita. "Take your time, dear."

"How long have I been asleep?"

"You weren't exactly sleeping."

"Drunk?" Rita asked.

Evie shook her head no. "You've been ill."

Rita's mind was clearing; now she remembered drinking the whiskey Evie had smuggled aboard the train. Yes, the whiskey. She'd been drugged! "Ill my ass," she murmured.

"What did she say?" Evie asked Ted.

"I think she's remembering things."

Rita attempted to sit up, but her head would not allow it.

"Take your time," Evie consoled.

"You slipped me a 'Mickey Finn,' goddamn you," Rita said, settling back on the pillow.

Evie looked away.

"My head weighs a ton," Rita continued.

"You'll be fine soon, Miss Gaspereaux," Ted said.

Rita turned her head on the pillow and strained her eyes to distinguish the details of Evie's face. "What have you done to me?"

"You've been safe all along," Ted said.

"What's he doing here, Evie?"

"He's my cousin," she answered. "Ted."

"Your cousin?"

Ted nodded.

"But how . . ." She stopped, unable to find the words.

"Evie and I have been working together," Ted explained. "From the beginning."

"Beginning?"

"The Fairmont lobby. Or before, actually."

Was this a nightmare?

"I'm sorry not to have introduced myself more honestly when we met in the club car," he continued. "A gentleman does not deceive. But I thought it best to reserve a few details of my identity, particularly in light of your . . . proposal."

"Proposal?" Rita asked, still foggy.

"Kansas City," he answered. "You were planning on ditching your 'prim cousin' Evie. I was to join you. Do you remember?"

This was all Cletus Gaspereaux's fault, Rita thought. He had taught her ninety percent of his business. But avoiding catastrophic coincidences, which real life seemed so intent to foist upon her, must have been contained in the other ten percent. "I don't know what you're talking about," she lied.

Ted turned to Evie. "Short-term memory."

Evie nodded. "Don't worry, Rita," she said. "All will be crystal clear in time. Just be patient."

"Why should I be patient with you?"

"I mean, be patient with yourself."

"We medicated you," Ted said. "You were taken ill."

"You drugged me."

Evie turned to her cousin. "Ted?"

He said nothing.

"I can't lie to her," Evie said.

Ted nodded, then turned to Rita. "Miss Gaspereaux, you're right. The truth is we took serious measures to ensure your arrival here. I'm sorry, but there seemed no other way."

"Where are we?"

"A stateroom," he answered.

"Yes, isn't it nice?" added Evie. "Second-class, with full deck privileges."

"Stateroom?"

"Yes," Evie said. "Well, a 'junior-stateroom.'"

"We're aboard a ship?"

Evie nodded.

Rita pulled herself into a half-sitting position. "What ship?"

"The S.S. *France*," Evie answered.

"What!"

"Yes, all is progressing quite nicely," Ted said.

"You've kidnapped me?"

"No, no," he answered. "'Kidnapping' is the removal of a person against his or her will to a location over which he or she has no control, for purposes of ransom or other nefarious intent."

"Exactly," Rita said.

"But that's not what we've done," he continued.

"I can scream," Rita said. "The steward will come running."

"Please don't. It'll accomplish nothing."

"You've kidnapped me!"

"Miss Gaspereaux, you agreed to accompany Evie on this trip for the purpose of acquiring the Black Falcon. And that's exactly what's happening now. Nothing more, nothing less."

"You slipped me a 'Mickey Finn,'" she said.

"That's just a detail, Miss Gaspereaux. The big picture remains the same."

Rita's brain pounded inside her skull.

"We apologize," he said. "We know it's unpleasant."

"But it's over now," Evie added.

"Then I'm free to leave?"

"Right now we're at sea," he said. "But when we reach land you may do what you please. You're not our prisoner."

"How long have I been unconscious?"

"From this point forward, we're going to play it straight with you," he said. "We're partners now, all the way."

"How long have I been out?"

"Days," he said.

"No, that's not possible."

"You were never in any danger."

"You weren't even unconscious the whole time," Evie added. "You were just kind of in and out. Maybe more 'out' than 'in,' but sometimes you were able to walk from one place to another and even answer questions. Going through customs, for example."

Customs? Rita remembered nothing after the Nevada border. "We're aboard a ship?" She had hoped the gentle swaying she felt beneath her was an aftereffect of whatever drug they had used on her. "How many days since we left San Francisco?"

"Six," Ted answered.

"That's not possible."

"Ted has some expertise in pharmacology," Evie said.

Rita closed her eyes. One can't lose six days . . . She was no fool.

This had to be a hoax. She straightened and pulled her legs over the side of the bed—fighting to keep her balance. She leaned toward Evie. "Why?"

Evie tried to speak, but no words came.

"We believe you're entitled to a share of the Falcon," Ted said.

Rita turned to him. "Who are you, really?"

He moved to her bedside, placing his hand on her hers, as if they were friends. "I'm Ted Bowman."

She removed her hand.

"My cousin's a professor at the University of California," Evie explained. "An archaeologist."

"So you really are a professor?"

"Yes."

"But you were never going to an academic conference?"

He shook his head no.

Rita turned to Evie. "So what's he doing here?"

"Last week, Sam asked me to go over to Berkeley and check with Ted to see if the story of the fourteenth-century knights and their bird statuette and all that other mystical stuff might be authentic."

"I told her it was quite possible," Ted interjected. "This is a rare opportunity, Miss Gaspereaux. Why, in my field . . ." He shook his head as if overwhelmed by the possibilities. "The value of this statuette is immense."

"Spare me the knights in shining armor jazz," Rita said.

"I'm glad to see you're getting your spirit back," Evie said.

"Don't speak to me as if you were my friend," Rita snapped at her. "Not after what you've done to me."

"Oh, it's far more than 'knights in shining armor jazz,' Miss Gaspereaux," Ted said.

She turned to him, her expression purposely blank.

"Of course, the statuette has enormous historical and artistic value in its own right," he continued, seeming to miss the impatience on her face. "Its origin dates to the depths of pre-history. But what makes the *objet d'art* truly priceless to collectors is the mythology that surrounds it. The idea that it is an ancient talisman that literally possesses wish-fulfilling powers for its owner. That's right, I said *literally*."

Rita shook her head no.

Ted took no notice but continued, as if lecturing in a seminar. "The Crusaders interpreted the source of the onyx statuette's mystical powers after their own fashion, but the true source of its power pre-dates Christ by many centuries. In ancient Sanskrit, a *cintamani* is a mystical stone that grants the mind its 'proper attainment.' The Black Falcon may be thought of as such a stone, though its origin likely predates even Sanskrit . . ."

Rita held up her hand. "That's enough. Stop."

He didn't. "The point is not whether the stone's powers are real. The point is that numerous wealthy collectors believe they are."

"This sounds like some sort of Sax Rohmer novel," she observed

"Don't worry," Evie answered. "Ted's an expert in the field. You can trust him."

"Like I trusted you?"

"I'm sorry, Rita. I meant you no harm. I've been straight with you all along."

"The whiskey?"

"I mean I've been straight in the important ways. Regarding the Falcon, for instance. And our willingness to share it with you."

"Then why drug me?"

Ted answered: "We had to ensure your arrival."

"You had no right."

"Perhaps not," Ted said. "But let me remind you of your plan to 'ditch' Evie, which you described to me in some detail."

Rita could hardly believe her bum luck. "I was never serious," she said. Her anger flared, though she had learned as a girl that anger compromised one's options. A real professional always managed her emotions. But she couldn't help herself. "You think I'd ever go off with some egghead like you?"

He looked away. "Maybe we overreacted."

"But there *was* that body in your bedroom," Evie added.

"I didn't kill him," Rita answered.

"And neither have we killed anybody," Ted said.

"Why don't you just tell me what you want?" Rita asked.

"The Falcon," they answered, almost in unison.

"I mean, what do you want from me?"

"Nothing difficult," Evie said.

"Just an introduction," Ted added.

"Where are we going?" Rita asked.

"Le Havre," Evie said, pointing to a porthole. "Outside is the Atlantic Ocean."

Rita closed her eyes.

"Your head will feel much better by dinner time," Ted said.

"The meals on board are very good," Evie added.

Rita opened her eyes. "And from Le Havre, where are we going?"

"You said, 'we,'" Evie observed. "Does that mean you've forgiven us?"

"No."

"We'll spend one night in Paris."

It was as she suspected. "And then?" She thought of Count Keransky.

"We'll find our objective there," Ted said.

Evie moved beside Rita. "So you're still interested?"

"Who are we going to see?" Rita pressed.

"Okay," Evie said. "Before dying in Sam's office, Captain Doyle whispered a man's name. He told me where I could find him. Poor, poor Captain Doyle. I still can't get his dying out of my mind."

"What does this have to do with me?"

"Captain Doyle said this man knew of you and that he'd be willing to talk to you."

"And that's why you kidnapped me?"

"As I explained before," Ted interrupted, "we haven't 'kidnapped' you—neither technically nor in the general sense of the word."

Rita dropped back to the pillow, her head too heavy to hold vertically anymore. She had no energy for an argument.

"All you need to know now is this," Ted continued. "Evie and I know the name of our contact. And our contact knows your name. Which makes us partners, because we need one another."

"You need me," Rita answered. "But I don't need either of you."

"Ah, but you don't know our contact's name," he said.

Keransky, she thought. But she kept her hand to herself. "Look, I don't need to know his name because I don't give a damn about getting the Falcon."

"Well, you're here now," Ted said. "What's to lose by playing along?"

Rita had had enough of these two. She needed a toilet and an aspirin and a hairbrush, a mirror and some running water and a toothbrush. "Where are my bags?" she asked.

Evie and Ted looked at one another.

"What is it?"

"We had trouble with customs in New York," Ted said.

"What?"

"Don't worry, Rita," Evie said. "We picked up toiletries and make-up and everything else you might need." She indicated a paper bag. "And when we get to Paris we'll buy you new clothes. Don't worry."

"What do you mean, you had a little trouble?"

Ted withdrew a claim check from his shirt pocket. "You can claim your bags on your return."

"In New York?"

Ted nodded. "The customs agents demanded that you personally declare the contents of your bag."

"But you couldn't make a declaration," Evie added, "Because you were sleeping."

"Sleeping?" Rita pressed.

"Well, you know what I mean."

"We had a hard enough time getting you on the ship," Ted added. "We had to leave your baggage behind."

"Why didn't you tell them the bags belonged to you?" Rita asked.

"Your name was on all the tags," Evie answered.

"Good God . . ."

"We managed to bring your book," Evie said. "I know how much you're enjoying it. I loved that section about Paul. Poor man, missing his dead brother so much . . . I knew you wouldn't want to leave it behind. So I hid it in my handbag. It's over there."

Rita said nothing.

"Really, you're very lucky," Evie continued. "Paris fashions are the best in the world. I wish *I* was getting new clothes."

"Go to Hell, Evie," Rita answered. It was not only her clothing that concerned her. She thought of Hollywood, receding with every white-capped mile. She had hoped to gain greater control of her life upon her father's death. But now her life had come loose from its moorings and she found herself literally adrift in the middle of the ocean.

Ted turned to Evie. "Why don't we give Rita a little time to herself?"

"In the closet, you'll find everything you need to dress for dinner," Evie said. "The steward helped us assemble an outfit for you. It's lovely."

"Dinner's at nine in the main dining room," Ted added. "We're registered as the 'Falcone' party."

"'Falcone?'"

He smiled. "Our assumed name."

"You're registered as our cousin," Evie added. "You're 'Rita Falcone.'"

"It's our *nom de guerre*," he continued. "Our little joke, eh?"

Rita shook her head.

"You will join us, won't you?" Evie asked.

"Of course she will," Ted observed. "She's on a ship in the middle of the Atlantic. Where else would she go?"

"Please leave me alone."

"Okay, we'll be on our way for now," Ted said.

"Yes, see you at dinner," Evie said.

When Rita heard the door to her cabin close, she dropped back to the bed, attempting to gather her thoughts.

All was a muddle.

At last, she arrived at this: she was being Shanghaied (second-class with full deck privileges) to Europe.

Who ever heard of such a thing?

And who'd believe that no one back in the States—or anywhere— even knew that she had been kidnapped? No one missed her. No one awaited her. Rita had not been raised like Rebecca of Sunnybrook Farm. She did not think of herself as sentimental, an emotion appropriate only for addled fat cats and over-the-hill whores. Ordinarily, she'd have greeted the world's indifference to her disappearance with relief, as it suggested independence. But now it felt different (an after-effect of the drugs they had given her?) It was almost sad. Hadn't Cletus Gaspereaux always at least kept track of her whereabouts? Didn't his locking her in their hotel suite prove that he had some concern for her?

Now, there was no one.

But ruminating got her nowhere.

She rose from the bed and made her way to the vanity where she sat before the mirror. Her face looked gaunt and pale.

Plotting was better than ruminating, she thought.

It made her feel at home, wherever she found herself.

Rita did not attend dinner at nine o'clock that night in the dining room on the Salon Deck of the S.S. *France*. She bolted her door and ignored the knocking and gentle calls ("Rita dear, are you all right?") that came from the hallway at midnight when Evie and Ted passed on their way back to their rooms. The next day, she slept late and spent the afternoon alone. Evie and Ted did not bother her. Eventually, she dressed in the borrowed gown she found in the closet; she sat at the vanity until the light through the porthole faded from sunlight to silver. Then she rang for the steward.

"Can you tell me how to get to the dining room?" she asked.

Her plan was as follows: Upon landing at Le Havre, she'd lose Evie and Ted (*after* somehow removing from their possession a proper restitution for her gross and unauthorized displacement—say, about four thousand five hundred dollars). She imagined them penniless in France—it pleased her. Then she would train up to the port of Antwerp and book return passage to New York and from there travel to Hollywood, sufficiently bankrolled to make a most impressive entrance into the glamorous world of the movie moguls. Perhaps she would claim to be a duchess or even a princess . . .

The Russian and the Falcon could rot.

"Ah, Rita, we're so happy you joined us," Ted said, rising from the large, round dinner table to greet her.

"I've joined you for dinner," she answered. "Nothing else."

"For now, that's quite enough," he said. "You look lovely."

"The dress fits you perfectly," Evie observed.

Rita hated the dress.

"This is our cousin," Ted announced to three middle-aged married couples who shared the table. The three gentlemen rose from their seats, offering niceties. The wives looked her up and down. They were all Americans, half finished with the soup course.

"We've been worried about you," Evie said.

"But we thought it best to leave you some time to yourself," Ted added.

"How are you feeling?" Evie asked.

Rita felt all right. "Terrible," she answered.

"Perhaps a good meal will help," Ted suggested.

"Maybe I could eat a little."

"That's a good girl," one of the husbands remarked, unaware of the glare his wife directed at him when his gaze remained too long on Rita's décolletage. "Did a flu bug get you down?" he asked.

"Some sort of treacherous little bugs got me down."

CHAPTER FOUR

T ed and Evie proved more difficult to rob and shake than Rita anticipated.

Naturally, Rita could not abandon them at sea—no going overboard; nonetheless, Ted and Evie hovered wherever she went, wary that if allowed even a moment of unsupervised time in the ship's smoking lounge or on the promenade deck or in the casino their "new friend" might form a partnership with one or another of the ship's only-too-eager-to-please male passengers and achieve an alternate alliance (which is exactly what Rita would have done if they were less vigilant). The dance became only more complex upon their disembarkation at Le Havre. There, Rita hoped to make away with the four grand and then elude them in the push and bustle of the Customs Office on the quay, but Ted took her hand and led her through the crowd like a protective beau, though his intent was more like a gendarme with a set of cuffs. She considered telling the customs officials that she had been kidnapped—but she was never comfortable trusting to police action. Meantime, Ted and Evie offered Rita little further information regarding plans for the next stage of their adventure. Rather, they had greeted her inquiries aboard ship with friendly, joking dismissals, as if to infer that discussing business details was beneath such trusted friends as they were fast becoming. Rita was not taken in, but as she harbored no intention of accompanying them to the end she did not press the point. On the train into Paris, Ted and Evie sat on either side of her in the club car, sipping aperitifs and talking nonsense, and when they climbed into the taxi cab at the Gare du Nord they again worked Rita into the middle.

At the Hotel Rouge on a side street just off the Boulevard Saint-Germain, Ted arranged for the "Presidential" suite—three bedrooms and, not incidentally, a heavy front door that could be dead-bolted to restrict passage out of the suite as well as in; thereafter, he made a show of slipping the old-fashioned key (brass and as long as a man's palm) onto a chain that he placed around his neck. "Isn't it lovely how Ted takes care of every little thing for us?" Evie asked Rita as they rode the elevator up to their suite.

"He's quite efficient," Rita answered.

Evie nodded. "Yes, that's the word everyone in our family uses to describe our Ted. Efficient."

"Please ladies," he said. "You're embarrassing me."

The porter, barely older than Rita and awkward in a gaudy red uniform far too large for his bony frame, opened the metal grill of the elevator and led them down the hall to their suite. "*Trois?*" he asked as he opened the door with his passkey (the existence of which Rita noted).

"Yes, there are three of us," Evie answered.

The porter grinned.

"What is it?" Evie asked him.

"Why not a one-bedroom suite?" he said, turning and winking at Rita. "More fun that way, eh?"

"What do you mean?" Evie asked.

The porter laughed. "Of course, if you need a fourth . . ."

Evie's jaw dropped.

"Look here, that's not respectful, *Monsieur*," Ted said. "You owe the ladies an apology."

The porter shrugged. "Okay, sorry. It was just a joke."

"I don't believe obscenities can be sloughed off as mere jokes," Ted said.

Rita thought sex was almost always laughable, but that Ted was right—it was no mere joke. It was too useful to be so easily dismissed, as it could be made to appear to be whatever one needed it to be. And now—as usual—sex (or its never-to-be-fulfilled promise) was shaping up as the most likely answer to Rita's immediate problem. She looked at the porter. He would be a snap to work. And he had a passkey. But how would she get alone with him? Even for five minutes, which is all it would take. She looked at Ted. Straitlaced and correct—he'd probably be even easier to crack than the kid, she thought.

"What a lovely room!" Evie said as she stepped inside.

"And the door can be locked to restrict passage both in and out?" Ted asked the porter.

"*Oui.*"

"Why does locking us in matter, Ted?" Rita asked.

"Security."

"Whose?"

"Ours. Remember, we're a team."

"Then shouldn't we come and go as we please? You, me, Evie . . . What if I should want a crêpe in the middle of the night?"

"That's not a good idea, Rita."

"Says who?"

"Me."

"And who do you think you are?"

He cleared his throat, set his shoulders, and spoke as if addressing a lecture hall. "From this point forward, ladies, we must operate as a single unit if we're going to succeed. We're very close to our objective, believe me. But we must move as one highly disciplined unit."

Rita looked at the porter, who still stood near the door with Ted and Evie's suitcases in hand. Ted seemed to have forgotten he was there. But Rita said nothing to stop Ted, even as he prattled on about security—what did any of it matter to her? She thought it was funny.

"We're like a crack unit of an army," he continued. "And all armies have generals. Just as all football teams have coaches and all businesses have presidents and . . ."

"Ted, I've had enough."

"Please let me finish, Rita."

"No, I've had quite enough," she said.

"Enough of what?"

"Of being ordered around in my life."

"Now, don't get me wrong, Rita. We're full partners, all the way. But..."

"But what?"

"He only has our best interests in mind," said Evie.

"Look, for the good of the team I've made some decisions," he said. "Now, I must admit that my natural impulse is to share decision-making. I pride myself on it. Actually, I've chaired numerous academic committees and I'm quite well regarded at the university for making every member's wishes count. Still, this is not a question of academic curriculum we're addressing here. We're no departmental committee. No, we're a raiding party. Determined, focused, unfazed by whatever dangers may lie ahead."

"Where shall I put the bags, sir?" the porter asked.

Ted did not seem to hear the boy. Rather, he continued: "Ladies, adventurers may have a reputation for mayhem. But consider the pirate films of Douglas Fairbanks. It's always the strength of a single pirate captain that enables his crew to prosper, true?"

Evie nodded. "Exactly."

"I like Douglas Fairbanks," the porter murmured.

Rita wondered what they were teaching these days at the University of California.

"Well, that's what I propose to do," Ted continued. "Be a leader. But don't worry, Rita. By this time tomorrow we'll have returned to democratic ways. Tomorrow or the next day. After we've acquired the Falcon. But for now I've concluded it's best for us to be together at all times in order to watch one another's back."

Rita knew whose back Ted intended to watch. "Even if what you say is true, about teams needing leaders . . . well, who made you leader?"

"I've organized this enterprise from the start."

"That's not true," she said. "Evie actually initiated all this. Right?"

"Well, technically yes."

"But I don't mind if he's the leader," Evie said. "He's good at planning."

"See?" he said to Rita.

"No, I don't see."

"Why don't we vote for a leader?" Evie asked.

"What?"

"That's democratic, right?" Evie continued.

"Who said anything about democracy?" Rita asked.

"All those in favor of making Ted leader raise your hand," Evie said.

"Are we in nursery school or something?" Rita asked.

Evie raised her hand.

Ted did likewise.

"That's two votes," Evie observed. "Those opposed?"

Rita raised her hand and glanced at the porter, who set the luggage on the floor. Sheepishly, he raised his hand as well.

"Don't be ridiculous," Evie said. "He's not on our team."

"Why are you still here?" Ted asked him.

"Okay, I'll be going," the porter said.

"Yes, you should go now," Ted said. "But I'm afraid I won't be giving you a gratuity, young man. Ordinarily, I always see to such things. But your disrespectful humor can't be ignored. To say nothing of your impudence. Voting in our election, for God's sake . . ."

The porter shrugged and left, closing the door after him.

"One doesn't talk to good, law-abiding Americans the way he did," Ted said as he dead-bolted the door with the key he wore around his neck. "Even a Frenchman should know better."

"Law abiding?" Rita asked.

"Sure. We haven't broken any laws, have we?"

"Aren't we here to steal the Falcon?"

"We don't know we'll have to steal it," he said. "Perhaps we'll come to an understanding with its owner. Maybe he'll sell it to us."

"Right, or maybe he'll give it to us as a 'welcome gift'?"

"But we've broken no laws."

"How about kidnapping?"

"Oh please, let's not start that again."

Rita had heard enough. She considered demanding to hold the room key to prove his trust of her. But she decided against it. He'd never bite.

Ted went to her. "Is it settled that we'll all stay together around the clock from now on, for safety's sake?"

"Sure," Rita said.

He extended his hand to shake. "No hard feelings?"

She shook his hand. She knew he noticed her missing finger, but he said nothing about it. If only he knew . . . But to her it was just a half-missing pinkie. She removed her hand from his, turned, and went to the window.

"How's the view?" Evie asked.

Looking out, Rita noted only that there was no fire escape. "Just peachy, Evie."

"Can you see the Eiffel Tower?"

"Yes and the Taj Mahal too."

"I suppose you ladies would like to wash before we go out for dinner?"

"We're going out?" Rita asked.

He shrugged. "Paris is reputed to be quite lovely by night."

Reputed—Rita loved it.

Downstairs in the hotel restaurant, dining on *coq au vin*, Rita pressed Ted and Evie to tell her more about their plan to acquire the Falcon (having endured a transcontinental train trip, an Atlantic crossing, and now a virtual house arrest in the Relais St. Germain district her curiosity was piqued, even if she had no intention of seeing their plan through). But Ted and Evie remained evasive. They drank their wine with frustrating moderation and assured Rita between courses that there was little to know beyond what they had already told her. "But I thought we were a team," Rita said. "Why should I be the only one in the dark?"

"Oh, you're not the only one," Evie said. "Ted hasn't told me the actual plan either."

"No?"

"But he's smart, Rita. Haven't you realized that yet? You can trust him."

"You haven't even told your cousin?" Rita asked him. "But she brought you news of the Falcon in the first place."

"I'm not keeping anything from her."

"No?"

He sighed, setting down his fork. "Let's just say the plan is still forming. I'm gathering intelligence for the actual assault. Or, in musical terms, you might think of what we'll be doing next as something of an improvisation."

"You mean you have no plan?"

"I didn't say that."

"Then what is it?"

He picked up his fork. "The sages of the Far East, truly wise men capable of marvelous feats, would doubtless suggest to us that the most enlightened thing we three could do at this moment would be to focus our attention on what we're actually here to do. That is, to be in the 'here and now.' We shouldn't be thinking about tomorrow or the day after, but should be aware of *this* moment, at *this* table. Notice, this is not a boardroom, nor is it a military planning room, nor is it a den of thieves. It's a 'dining' room, ladies. So let's dine."

"The *coq au vin* is delicious," Evie said.

Rita thought Ted worked his con game with a certain skill. Unless it was no game but was just what it appeared to be—incompetence.

No matter.

Later, walking along the Seine smoking cigarettes after the evening had turned to night, Ted and Evie kept Rita not only within sight but within their physical grasp. She'd not have guessed they were capable of such consistent and determined effort. Of course, she might have broken into a run at any time. But she hadn't their money yet. Besides, she considered such a maneuver beneath the dignity of a true confidence artist; sprinting into the shadows and away from trouble suited only boorish muggers and clumsy second-story men. Hadn't Gaspereaux taught her that one's mind was the only weapon one should ever rely on, always disparaging tales of physical boldness (of course, what choice did he have, being so fat and ill-disposed toward physicality)? And there was something else that kept Rita from dodging down one or another of the dimly lit side streets that led down to the river, something she had not immediately recognized when she first encountered it two nights before at dinner with Ted and Evie aboard ship, something that even now she did not trust enough to name. Surely, Ted and Evie were not her friends. But for short stretches (punctuated by much longer periods of disdain and aggravation) Rita found herself almost enjoying their company.

Foolishness, of course.

"The boys in the administration building will sure be surprised by this lowly archeology professor," Ted said as they walked under a bridge and emerged along the river just across from the Notre Dame Cathedral. "They think so little of us, you understand. We're supposed to be mere tweed-coated incidentals to their larger academic plans. Oh, they get buildings named after them, along with the donors, while *we* do all the actual research and teaching and we don't even get tenure. Hell, if a guy in my position makes just one little mistake, even in a privately published tract on, say, the Peloponnesian War . . . Well, you'd think I'd gone and killed Pericles myself or something."

"Ted is a wonderful teacher," Evie added.

"Wait 'til they see me drive up to the administration building in a brand new Pierce-Arrow," Ted said. "Oh, they'll do a double-take that'll snap their necks. And wait until I hand over a check for ten grand. Or maybe twenty grand . . . I could endow a chair. Yeah, that'd really teach the bastards!"

"You'd give them money?"

He smiled. "What sweet revenge."

Rita didn't understand academia.

"I wonder what Sam Hammett would say if he knew that at this moment I was actually walking along the River Seine?" Evie asked. "Here it is a moonlit night and here I am within sight of the Notre Dame Cathedral, which is *so* much lovelier in person than it is in photographs. You think he'd believe it? Me, his secretary, who most times he thought barely capable of buying him a sandwich . . ."

"That's not true, Evie," Ted said. "I met Sam. He thought the world of you."

"Maybe. But I doubt he believed I could manage something like this."

"Few could," Ted said. "But you did."

Evie gestured toward the cathedral. "It's so . . . big."

Rita had seen Notre Dame before. She had been inside. But she did not begrudge Evie's enthusiasm.

"Sam himself has never been here," Evie continued. "Not even as a tourist, let alone as an adventurer, as we are. Oh, he used to talk plenty about Paris. On slow days in the office he'd go on and on about all the culture and the women and the gourmet food. But he's not here now. No, it's just us three. Wait 'til he hears about it! He'll turn green with envy."

"You think it's a good idea to tell him what we've done?" Rita asked, ignoring what she knew: that Evie's Parisian adventure was not going to end in such a way that she would want to brag about it to anyone.

"He's trustworthy," she said.

"Now let's not get carried away," Ted said. "We'll decide who we're going to tell what, later."

"Oh Ted," Evie said. "Ever the cautious one."

"Cautious and efficient . . ." Rita mused. "Mr. Excitement."

"In our line of work you can't afford to be reckless," he said.

"So now we share a 'line of work'?" Rita asked.

"I wonder what Sam would say about all this if he *were* with us," Evie said. "You know, walking along with us."

"You mean about the Falcon?" Ted asked.

"No, I mean about the river. If he were here. You know, with the moon so bright and all. And the lights in the trees. And that lovely bridge over there. The Pont Neuf? And the barges on the water, like those over there, and all the music from the *bal-musettes*."

"He'd like it," Ted said.

"And the cafés," Evie continued. "I wonder what he would drink. Espresso in those little cups? I guess I'm just wondering what he'd make of a night like this in a place like this. That's natural enough, isn't it?"

Rita noticed tears in Evie's eyes. What a sucker she was for this Sam. This Dashiell. This gumshoe turned aspiring novelist. Then she thought of a scene she had just read in her novel, *Dorothy G., Kansas*, which coincidentally featured an American private detective working in Paris . . .

❖

Paul's office consisted of a single, dimly lit attic room five stories above the Boulevard du Montparnasse. On the directory downstairs:

Paul Darnell
Investigateur Privé
Personnes Disparues
#5A

The room's ceiling sloped down at a steep angle from the interior wall across to a single, gabled window through which Paul had spent more hours these past months than he cared to consider watching men in straw boaters and women in all manner of sleek *chapeaux* moving up and down the boulevard with what seemed to Paul a vitality in their steps that he feared his own movements were coming to lack. Work was sporadic at best for an American private investigator in Paris (particularly one who carried a city guidebook strapped to his ankle where more hardened detectives carried Derringers). The desk and chair took up most of the attic room, leaving space only in one corner for a metal filing cabinet and in another for a three-foot-wide antique globe that Paul had bought at a flea market in the Latin Quarter shortly after his arrival in Paris. On the wall behind the desk hung a framed photograph of Joe, who Paul described to his clients as his brother and former partner. He didn't tell them that Joe was also a missing person. Or that he would likely always be a missing person. That way he didn't have to acknowledge that it didn't take a Sigmund Freud to figure that Paul's specialty was likely a result of his brother's disappearance.

"You're a private detective?" the pretty young woman asked.

"I'm Paul Darnell." He waited for her to introduce herself.

But she only shook her head, as if unsure of her own name. "I've come in search of a missing person," she said.

"You've come to the right place . . ."

❖

Rita was ripped from her reverie about the characters Dorothy and Paul first meeting and was returned to the stroll along the river by a question from Ted: "Don't you agree, Rita?"

"Agree with what?"

"Agree that Evie's boss Sam would be downright lucky to be in her company on a night like this? Just as we're lucky, right?"

Rita said nothing.

"He's a dope for not appreciating you properly, Evie," Ted continued.

Evie wiped at her eyes, smudging her make-up.

Rita took a hankie from her handbag and handed it to her.

"Thank you, Rita."

Rita thought that if ever there was a doomed motive for a confidence game it was unrequited love. Or professional spite. But that didn't matter—this wasn't her game.

Ted took Evie's hand. "After we've got the Falcon and we're safely home, you can tell Sam all about it. Don't you think that'll be all right, Rita?"

"Sure."

Evie smiled. "After we have the Falcon … After we're millionaires … Well, maybe then I won't want to tell him."

"Maybe we should make our way back now," Ted said.

As they entered the hotel lobby, which at this hour was quiet, Ted and Evie revealed to Rita the "plan" (or what passed for a plan). It was this: the following afternoon they would call at the home of the Russian.

"Will he be expecting us?" Rita asked.

"No."

"But he'll see us?"

Ted nodded.

"Who is this Russian anyway?"

"Who he is doesn't matter," Ted said. "It's who you are that counts."

"I don't understand."

"Tell her, Evie," Ted said.

"The poor ship captain …" Evie said. "Two weeks ago … In Sam's office. Just before he died … With his last breath … No one around but me …"

"Finish a goddamn sentence," Rita said.

"He said, 'Count Keransky in Paris will know the Gaspereaux girl.'"

"Which is why we're here, the three of us," Ted added.

"Me? Why me?" she asked, wondering if Ted and Evie knew about the father thing.

"We don't know," Evie said. "But that's what the poor ship captain said. And dying men have no reason to lie, do they?"

Everyone has reason to lie, Rita thought. "What else did he say?"

"He told me where we can find Keransky," Evie said.

"Where?" Rita asked.

Evie started to answer, but Ted stopped her.

"Don't worry about exact locations," he said. "We know our way around."

Sure you do, Rita thought.

They crossed the hotel lobby toward the elevator.

"Once we've made the acquaintance of Keransky," Ted continued, "We'll play it by ear."

"You'll just pick out the tune?" Rita asked.

"In a manner of speaking."

Rita shook her head no. "This sort of thing is not exactly like music."

Ted shrugged. "What I mean is that we'll enter his home and reconnoiter, then we'll withdraw to our hotel, consult, and only *then* will we plan a final assault on the Falcon."

"Assault? When did you become Douglas Fairbanks?" Rita asked.

"He's just being melodramatic," Evie said.

The elevator arrived and they stepped inside. The evening had been pleasant enough—actually, Rita would not have minded spending another day or two with Ted and Evie, if circumstances allowed. She was no recluse, however she had been raised. But time together was out of the question now—soon Ted and Evie would attempt to use Rita to gain access to the Russian. And who could blame them? They were as human as anybody. Rita knew how relationships worked, however chummy they might make a girl feel from time to time. Hell, Emil Madrid had always been an entertaining companion—and yet

Rita knew how quickly he'd have sold her out if the opportunity arose. Consider their last meeting. It was human nature. And she knew Gaspereaux would have told her she'd be foolish to remain in Ted and Evie's company one moment longer than necessary, especially in light of what she had obtained on their last day at sea aboard the S.S. *France*. Then, Ted had locked her into his stateroom for five minutes while he paid off the steward and two French immigration officers. Briefly alone among his things, she riffled through his suitcase. Unfortunately, she failed to find the money, which he likely kept on his person, but did discover the stash of chloral hydrate used to drug her. She had pocketed it by the time he returned. More subtle than a gun, the drug was a powerful tool. She had hoped she wouldn't have to use it against them, but Ted and Evie proved more disciplined in their attentions than she had expected and now there was no time left for other options.

"Rita's right, Ted," Evie said, grinning. "'Assault' may be a little too strong a word. You're not exactly the Scarlet Pimpernel."

"I didn't say that," Rita snapped, initiating her final maneuver.

"What?"

"Please don't twist my meaning, Evie."

Evie was confused.

"Look, Ted has gotten us this far," Rita said, reversing the flippancy she had shown toward him from the start. "He's proved himself to be a remarkable man. At least that's how he seems to me. I mean, everything's worked out for the best, right? It's true that I had my moments of doubt. Who wouldn't, considering the circumstances I woke up to find myself in? But now I trust him to get us all the way to the Falcon."

Ted turned to her, surprised. "Well, thank you, Rita."

"So don't underestimate your cousin, Evie," Rita continued.

"But *you* made the joke about Fairbanks . . ."

"It was no joke," Rita interrupted. She turned to Ted, her tone softening. "When *did* you become Douglas Fairbanks?"

He didn't know what to say.

"Thank you, Ted," Rita continued. "You took me away from a grieving place and delivered me to this . . . adventure."

He shrugged. "Oh, I'm no Doug Fairbanks."

Rita continued: "What you may not understand, Ted, is that no one has ever understood me before. Not my father. Nor any of his acquaintances, who were all bastards, though as a child I thought of them as my family. Pathetic, isn't it? But I had no one to compare them to. I didn't know friendship."

"You've led a lonely life," Ted said.

"I understand that now, Ted, because you treated me as a friend. I can't describe to you what that means. Thank you."

"You're welcome," Evie said.

Rita ignored her. "And I want you to know something, Ted. I've watched you these past few days and I know you'll get us through."

He attempted to fend off a smile. "Now, don't forget about Evie."

Rita turned to her. "Oh, dear, dear Evie . . ."

"This elevator is starting to feel a little crowded," Evie said.

Rita touched Ted's cheek with her fingers as if to confirm the accuracy of Evie's observation.

"I thought you didn't like me," Ted said.

"I didn't like what you did to me back in the States."

He shook his head, regretfully. "If I'd known your true character then, as I do now . . ."

"I understand, Ted. I forgive you."

The elevator arrived at the fourth floor.

"When, exactly, did you become so amenable to my cousin?" Evie asked as they stepped out onto their floor. "Seems sudden."

"Tonight."

"Why?"

"Because, unlike most men, he's not all talk."

Evie looked doubtful. But that didn't matter. She wasn't the mark. And Ted was buying every word. Men were easy.

"Well, we all have a big day tomorrow," Evie said. "I suggest we get a good night's rest."

"Sure," Ted said. "Big day."

Rita said nothing.

Ted unlocked the door to their suite.

Rita moved to the sidebar, where the liquor bottles stood. "Can I pour a nightcap for anyone?"

Ted shook his head no.

"Sure, maybe one," Evie said.

Rita palmed the vial of chloral hydrate that she had been carrying with her all night. What dosage? All that mattered was that it be strong enough to do its work. She slipped a third of the vial into Evie's drink, which she turned and handed to the heartsick secretary. "Down the hatch, my dear," she said. "You deserve a good night's rest."

Evie took the drink.

Yes, this Mickey Finn business was devious. But effective.

Shortly thereafter, the three adjourned to their bedrooms. It was simple enough for Rita to convey with a glance in Ted's direction how the rest of their night would go. He need only wait for her to come to him. Inside her bedroom, Rita sat on the window seat, marking time on her wristwatch as she watched the street below gradually empty of pedestrians. She hummed a song that the dance band on the S.S. *France* had played mid-Atlantic. She picked up her novel, flipping through the last chapter she'd read, wherein Dorothy had moved from New York to Paris and made the acquaintance of the bereaved American detective, Paul Darnell, who had opened a one-man private detective agency. Now, the two fictional characters were spending a glamorous first evening together.

❖

Dorothy took Paul's offered hand as they pressed into the feathered and floral-scented crowd that mingled outside the entrance to the

Théâtre des Champs-Elysées. Twenty minutes to show time. Paul did not pull at Dorothy as they moved, but led her gently through the crowd as if navigating up a rocky stream. She liked the way her hand felt in his, even if his palm was a trifle damp. His nervousness did not bother her. Likewise, she did not mind that Paul sometimes stumbled on his own words; the words had proved always worth waiting for. And she appreciated that his manner contradicted the common habit among so many expatriates of playing at either a dissolute martyrdom or an unshakable machismo. Paul was the real thing. In a city of artists and poseurs, authenticity was more precious than genius. She considered it additionally revealing that earlier that evening over aperitifs Paul had told boyhood stories of his brother Joe rather than spinning any of the self-aggrandizing tales of intrigue set in the dark alleys of the Quarter that a less sincere man in his profession would doubtless have found irresistible as "seductive" material. In all, Dorothy trusted that Paul was just what he appeared to be: a man at once both bold and decent in a way that she had begun to fear did not exist anymore outside the pages of over-long nineteenth-century novels.

He pressed toward the ticket window.

"How did you get these tickets, Paul?" she asked as the attendant handed him an envelope. "I heard it was nearly impossible."

"A friend," he answered. "Georges. We can meet him after the show, if you'd like. For dinner. He's a good sport." He looked at his wrist-watch. "Do you want to have a smoke before we go in?"

"Sure."

They moved back through the loitering crowd to the sidewalk, which was bathed a flickering red and yellow by the marquee lights above. The air smelled of Turkish blend tobacco. Beyond, the glimmering boulevard teemed with taxis that squawked and sputtered and sped, headlights gleaming. Dorothy leaned toward Paul as he lit her cigarette. "The review said Josephine Baker is fantastic," she said.

Paul nodded. "That's what I've heard too."

She glanced up to the giant poster above the entrance. Small copies of the picture had been plastered for weeks on every kiosk in Paris, which was much taken with the "Ebony Venus" and her dance, the Charleston, which locals pronounced *Shar-less-tawn*. Dorothy turned to Paul. "Did you know Josephine Baker owns a pet leopard?" she asked. "It was in the *Herald Tribune*."

"Chiquita," Paul said.

"What?"

"That's the leopard's name."

"Oh."

"And she keeps a snake called Kiki," he continued. "She wears it around her neck when she goes out some evenings."

"A snake? Rousseau would like that."

Paul nodded. "She says it helps her to separate the men from the boys."

"How do you know all this?"

"My friend Georges. He's very close to Josephine."

"You have exciting friends, Paul."

"A few. But this isn't my real life."

"What do you mean?"

"Well, all this . . ." He searched for the word, then indicated with a sweep of his hand all that lay about them. "These tickets, these lights this . . . glamour."

"Not your 'real' life? I don't understand. Are you being unreal with me, Paul?"

"No, no. I wouldn't say unreal."

"Deceptive?" she asked.

"No. In fact, that's what I'm trying to avoid right now, Dorothy. Being deceptive."

"I don't understand."

"Well, my friend Georges arranged for these tickets. He knows just about everybody. He's a pretty sophisticated guy, a bit of a cad, actually, but at heart he means no harm. Of course, his wife might disagree from time to time about that."

"He's married?""

Paul nodded.

"And not to Josephine Baker," she said.

"That's right."

"But he and Josephine . . ."

"Yeah."

"Do you know his wife?"

Paul shook his head no.

Dorothy took a long drag on her cigarette. "From time to time I forget we're in Paris," she said. "That we're 'moderns' and all that."

He nodded. "I don't know how modern this 'mistress' thing actually is."

"That's true."

"But you're right, we're not in Kansas anymore."

"You're not married are you, Paul?"

"No, no," he said. "Please, don't get me wrong, Dorothy. Georges' life, his infidelities—well, they're not the sort of thing I want for myself. Still, it can be quite illuminating to observe. He's very engaged in his world. Theatrical openings, illicit liaisons and all that. Myself, I don't do those things very often. That's all I'm trying to say."

"No illicit liaisons?"

He laughed. Then he gestured about the well-heeled crowd and the glittering theatre. "I mean this sort of thing too."

"Do you dislike 'this sort of thing'?"

"The revue?"

She nodded.

"No, no, it's great," he said. He tossed the butt of his cigarette into the gutter. "I'm no anarchist or socialist, you understand. I'm all for good times. It's just, well, I mean, I'm not really in the fast set, if you want the truth, Dorothy. I hope you understand that, for whatever it's worth."

"My best friend lives in New York," Dorothy explained. "Nancy Bing. She's an artist. And also a waitress. Mostly a waitress. Actually, one hundred-percent waitress, if you judge by her income. We worked together in a tea room back in the Village. We had lots of fun. And heartache too, which comes with the territory. Being young, I mean. Such drama."

"Sure."

"It helps to have a friend who's always on your side," Dorothy continued. "That's Nancy. Is Georges your best friend?"

"You could call him that. But we're not like brothers or anything."

"That's too bad."

"It's all right. It frees me up."

"For what?"

"My investigations. One in particular."

"Which one?"

"I'll tell you about it another time, okay?"

"Okay."

"Georges plans to write mystery novels," Paul said. "We meet for drinks once in a while. I tell him my crime tales of the Left Bank, half of which are as fictionalized as anything he'll ever write. But the stories I tell him buy me drinks the way Scheherezade's stories bought her time. Of course, Georges is full of stories himself. So I buy him plenty of drinks too."

"Do you like mystery novels?"

"Arséne Lupin."

"Ah, you like the villain who gets away with the crime."

"I don't know if I'd call Lupin a villain."

"No?"

"Well, he's a master thief. A criminal, that's for sure. But that's not always the same thing as a villain."

"That's true. Some of the most law-abiding citizens . . ." She stopped.

He nodded. "See, what I like about Lupin is that he's willing to sacrifice all he's ever acquired in his crimes, which is quite a lot, to save one of his own. His people mean more to him than his wealth. That's what makes him noble. Like in *The Crystal Stopper*. Have you read that one?"

She shook her head no.

"Well, in *The Crystal Stopper* one of his younger accomplices is actually led to the steps of the guillotine before Lupin is able to rescue him. How's that for the 'nick' of time? For most of the book, it looks pretty hopeless for the boy, a petty thief who's been falsely accused of murder. But through it all, the reader knows that Lupin will go to the guillotine himself, if necessary, to save the boy. See, Lupin's a rascal, but his instincts are good."

"So you like it when the good-at-heart get away with their crimes?"

"Who doesn't?"

"Like your friend Georges?"

Paul shrugged. "I'm a detective, but I'm no Inspector Javert."

"I never thought you were," she said. "Besides, you'd look very silly in one of those tri-cornered hats."

He laughed.

The crowd had begun to enter the theatre.

He turned toward the theatre entrance, then took her hand once more.

"Champagne?" Paul asked as they entered the lobby of the theatre.

"Yes," she answered. "Much champagne. Much."

A few minutes later, they took their seats in the theatre.

The house lights dimmed. On the curtained stage, three spotlights came together to make a circle of white intensity.

The Revue:

First, jazz pounded and beat and simmered. Then the curtain rose. Dorothy sat up in her chair as Josephine Baker entered spread-eagled, draped over a male dancer's shoulders. She was naked but for a tiny skirt of flamingo feathers. Her skin shimmered like satin. She slid from the dancer's body in time to the jazz syncopation, lingering for a moment about his long, muscular legs, then stood, shimmying with a sensual exuberance the likes of which Dorothy had never before witnessed on a stage (or anywhere else, for that matter).

"What do you think, Paul?" Dorothy asked, shouting over the din.

"I think Josephine has a future in this town."

Miss Baker spun across the stage, her shoulders shimmying, her hands as lively as birds. She stopped at the edge of the proscenium. Stillness. The music stopped. A silent moment—not more than three seconds, which seemed like three minutes. The audience held its breath then roared encouragement, unable to remain silent any longer. Then a light-hearted piano. Then the jazz band. A new, Caribbean rhythm. Josephine smiled, then began to sing, her voice reedy and thin but rich with a character that was at once erotic and comic.

When she rolled her hips—a saxophone riff.

The shimmy of her breasts—coronets soaring.

The toss of her arms—a blast of trombones.

Meantime, her smile seemed to acknowledge both the sexuality of her dancing and the ironic wit of its presentation. (A flamingo feather skirt!) Dorothy discovered herself wanting not only to watch Miss Baker, but to be her—if not for a lifetime, then at least for an hour or two every day.

Or better yet, every night.

After the show, Paul and Dorothy took a cab down the wide, tree-lined avenue—through the almost empty Place de la Concorde and the shadowy Jardin des Tuileries—and crossed the river to the Quarter, which teemed. Paul pointed to a café called Byron. He paid the driver. Dorothy stepped onto the boulevard. Here, the night smelled of licorice, orange blossom, and petrol. From a *bal-musette* across the street came the clattering notes of a piano, accompanied by drums and thumping bass. On the opposite corner, the sidewalk outside *Le Dome* was crowded with expatriates, some of whom Dorothy was bound to know, none of whom she wanted to see right now. She was happy with things as they were.

Paul took her hand. "Hungry?" he asked.

"Sure."

"Thirsty?"

"Why not?"

"We'll start with a St. Rafael?" he suggested. "Then with dinner we'll drink the *vin ordinaire*, which is not ordinary at all."

"Okay, nothing ordinary for us," she said

The proprietor of the Café Byron, a bearded man named Josephe, brought drinks in two glasses that he set before Dorothy and Paul at their tiny table in the corner of the dark room. Over the *foie gras* and then the chestnut and celery soup, Dorothy explained why Anatole France was one of her favorite writers:

"First," she said. "His name. France."

"That was his pen name," Paul said.

"Doesn't matter," she answered. "If you've taken the name of a country for your own, especially this one, you must be pretty good."

He laughed. "Okay."

Dorothy liked the way she felt about herself when she was with this man. "My favorite of his books used to be *The Crime of Sylvestre Bonnard*," she said.

"I haven't read that one."

"It's about a man who selflessly raises the orphaned daughter of a woman who years before broke his heart. He cares for the girl as if she's his own, though he knows she's the daughter of his rival. But jealousy doesn't matter to Sylvestre Bonnard. His heart is as deep as the sea. Isn't that lovely?"

"Yes. But it's not your favorite anymore?"

"No. Now I prefer *Revolt of the Angels*."

"I know that one," he said.

"I like that the guardian angels want to overthrow their boss, the 'Big Man' upstairs," she continued.

"But they fail."

"Doesn't matter," she said. "I respect their courage. And I envy it."

The next afternoon, Dorothy wrote a long letter to her friend Nancy Bing, a portion of which follows:

> ... *So after dinner we went to his flat, which is just off the Boulevard Saint-Germain across a narrow street from a music hall called Le Raton Bleu from which we heard jazz played until almost dawn. His place has a large skylight and a window that almost fills one wall. Paul keeps photographs of his family (parents and one deceased brother) on his desk. He had a few racing forms from Auteuil set on one chair. Across the inside wall was a bookshelf crowded with histories of the Great War, mysteries, and a whole shelf of novels borrowed from Sylvia Beach's lending library ...*

❖

Rita stopped reading when she heard Evie begin to snore in the next room. She thought it must be nice to be so clearheaded that sleep came easily (of course, the dose of chloral hydrate didn't hurt the process any, either). Regardless, the carefree days were almost over for Evie. What awaited was destitution in France for her and her cousin. It was nothing less than they deserved. Rita stood and slipped out of her bedroom and into the sitting room. She tried the front door, which Ted had indeed locked behind them. She went to Ted's bedroom. She did not knock, but opened his door and walked in. A candle burned on the vanity table and she could see him sitting up in the bed in monogrammed pajamas. The chain with the key glistened around his neck.

"Rita?"

"Not sleeping yet?" she whispered.

He shook his head no.

"Funny," she said. "I couldn't sleep myself. Perhaps, since we're both awake, we should be awake together."

"Sure."

She said nothing.

"Would you like to sit down?" he asked.

She went to his bed and sat on the end.

"Did you come here to talk?"

"Not exactly. I came to be with you."

"You mean as we are now?" he asked.

"Sure." He was no Valentino. "And maybe even more together."

"Oh, that's quite an idea."

"An idea is just something in your head," she said. "I'm talking about more than just something in your head."

He said nothing.

She leaned toward him.

He swallowed hard. "Rita, you're a bold girl."

"That's not a bad thing is it?"

He shook his head no.

"I'm just a girl who knows what she wants," she said.

"And this is what you want?"

"Would I be here otherwise?"

"Well, you haven't actually had much choice about being here, seeing as you were . . . kidnapped."

She smiled. "Legally speaking, I wasn't actually kidnapped."

He laughed. "Glad you see it that way."

"Unless, of course, you want to *pretend* I'm your captive."

His grin vanished. "Well, that's quite an idea . . ."

"More than just an idea."

"Rita, there's something I have to make you understand before we go any further."

"Hush," she said. Sometimes talk brought men back to their senses—she didn't want that.

"But there's something I need to make perfectly clear. It's . . ."

"The candle is a nice touch," she interrupted.

He sat up straighter. "Actually, I burn a candle every night."

"In the event that I might come to you like this?"

"Actually, I don't like to go to sleep in the dark."

"You're kidding."

"No."

"Ted, you didn't have to tell me that."

He shrugged. "I'm honest, Rita."

"Are you?"

He nodded.

Maybe he was, she thought. Wouldn't that be something? Of course, she could not afford to take any chances. If he was an honest man—well, that was his problem. "You don't want me to leave, do you?"

"No, Rita. But . . ."

"But?"

"Well, there's something I have to tell you."

"Go ahead."

"I have a girl back home."

She waited, but he said nothing more. At last she prodded: "And?"

"Well, I just thought you should know."

"That's it?"

He nodded.

"What's her name?"

"Trudy."

"Do you want me to help her with her make-up or something?" she asked.

He laughed, nervously. "Of course not."

"So why are you telling me?"

He struggled to find the words.

"Hush, Ted." She could not allow his ineptitude to spoil the moment and thereby spoil the plan. "It's all right. I'm moved by your honesty."

He took a deep breath, composing himself.

She smiled. "Let me get this straight. You're telling me that you're not going to be able to make an honest woman of me?"

"That's a hard way of putting it, Rita."

"Do you think I want to be an 'honest' woman?"

"No?"

She looked into his eyes. "This is about you and me, here and now. It's not about the past. It's not about other places or people. And it needn't be about the future either, if you don't want it to be. Remember what you said tonight about the Eastern mystics? 'Being in the moment' and all that? My goodness, those Buddhist monks must lead wild lives!"

"Actually, they don't."

"Well, so much for Buddhism."

He laughed.

Rita had him now—she had learned long before that if a pretty girl can get a man to laugh, she can get whatever she wants.

"I just wanted you to understand a thing or two about me," he said.

"I already know all I need to know."

"Which is?"

"You're a man of action, disguised as a man of intellect." Nice words, she thought. Good enough to remember for future use.

"Einstein with a gun, eh?"

"Do you carry a gun?" she asked. Now that would surprise her.

"I meant metaphorically."

"Oh, that kind of a gun . . ." She moved toward him across the bed. "Is your metaphorical gun loaded, Professor Einstein?"

He swallowed hard and nodded.

She kissed his lips and in the process of moving against him felt beneath the covers that his gun was indeed loaded. "Wait," she said, pulling back.

"What is it?"

Things had gone far enough, she thought. There was no sense overdoing the Theda Bara routine—especially as she didn't actually need to go through with the thing. Rather, a touch now of Mary Pickford reticence . . . "Oh Ted, this is all happening so fast."

He looked at her, confused.

"My heart is hungry," she said. "But my head . . . Oh, it's spinning so."

"That's not a bad thing, is it?"

"No, of course not. But would you think me a coward if . . ."

"If what, dear?"

She looked away, shy. "If I had a brandy to calm my nerves?"

"Sure, of course," he said, but she saw a shadow of doubt cross his face.

"Please don't misunderstand," she added. "It's not as if I do this often. I need the drink because I'm not a Vamp."

"Of course not."

"This is a very special moment for me."

"Me too."

"You're such a dear."

"Whatever makes you comfortable," he said.

"The brandy is in the sitting room."

"Let me get it for you," he said.

"No, I'll go." She climbed off the bed. "You stay there."

"Okay."

"Would you like me to get a drink for you too?" she asked.

"Why not?" he said.

There was one damn good reason "why not," she thought.

Now, she moved out of his room and crossed the dark sitting area of the suite to the place she had hidden the vial. She would prepare two glasses of brandy. One straight, the other spiked—she'd give him a taste of his own medicine. The irony pleased her. She glanced back toward Ted's bedroom, where she heard him shuffling in the bed sheets. She did not want him following her out here. Hurriedly, she slipped the cap off the vial. How much constituted a good dose? She needed him out cold, fast. And he was bigger than Evie.

"Are you all right out there?" he called to her in a whisper from the bedroom.

She had no time to dwell on the dosage, so she poured it all into his glass.

"Coming, dear," she whispered.

She hesitated. What if he actually intended to share with her whatever booty he and Evie managed to acquire from the Russian? She wouldn't put it past him, the fool. Then she stopped herself—what rot was she thinking? Ted and Evie would never acquire the Falcon; rather, they would acquire only trouble for themselves. Hadn't they already done so by dragging Rita into their scheme—who but fools would pack as live a minx as she into their own luggage? And if Rita stayed among them for even another day, their ineptitude would likely bring the law (or worse) down upon her head as well as theirs. And as for Ted being an honest man . . . well, honest my ass, she thought. Sure, he had made a point of telling her about his girl back home—his faithful Trudy. But would he ever tell Trudy what he had done here in Paris with Rita? Of course, if Rita got the dosage in his drink right there would be nothing for him to confess except thwarted lasciviousness. He deserved the mind-bending headache that would await him tomorrow when he awoke. She turned back toward the bedroom, a glass of brandy in each hand.

She stopped in the doorway.

To keep from confusing which hand held the spiked drink, she concocted the following pneumonic: after drinking, he would be *left* behind. Her plan: after he lost consciousness, she would remove the room key from around his neck; next she would riffle their luggage, the chest of drawers, even under sofa cushions and the mattresses if necessary to find the forty-five hundred, or however much of it was left; then she would use the room key to let herself out of the suite, slipping downstairs and away from the hotel. She figured she would have at least until sunrise before Ted and Evie awoke from their chloral hydrate dreams. By then, she would be long gone, on to her new and well-financed life. And Ted and Evie would be broke and friendless in Paris (an admonishing but important lesson for both).

She returned to the bedroom and to the edge of Ted's bed.

"Here's your drink, my turtledove."

He took the glass and proposed a toast. "To romance."

"What a lovely and original sentiment."

They drank and talked sweet nothings, fondling and kissing but doing little else. Ted was out cold in less than ten minutes. Faster even than she had hoped . . .

But something was wrong.

Ted had seemed to stop breathing.

"Ted? Ted?" Concerned, Rita slapped his face.

She put her ear to his chest. No heartbeat. No breathing. She sat up and pounded on his heart as she had once seen a fire captain do for a victim of smoke inhalation. (Had she given him too much of the drug? But how was she to know the proper dosage? It was Gaspereaux who always slipped drugs to rivals who came into and out of their lives.)

Finally, she whispered Ted's name into his ear, as if that could bring him back. Over and over. Emphatic. Imploring. Then she was no longer whispering but speaking his name aloud, heedless of who might hear.

But he was gone.

She stood and backed away from the bed. Oh, he may have been an aggravating hypocrite, but she'd never intended to *kill* him. He was too foolish to deserve that. Death was for the likes of her father and his cohorts. The knowing operators of the world. The predators. Not naïfs. Even avaricious ones. But what could Rita do about it now? Call for help? That would not bring him back but only invite questions. And she had learned long before that questions were always to be avoided. So, she backed away farther from the bed, wondering now if she may have slipped too much of the drug into Evie's drink as well.

She raced into the secretary's bedroom.

Evie was in a deep sleep . . . but breathing. Shallow but steady breaths. She would be all right.

Relieved, Rita settled into the chair beside Evie's bed.

Oh, what a terrible world Evie would awaken to.

But Rita hadn't time for self-recrimination.

After all, hadn't Ted and Evie chosen to play a devious and dangerous game?

And wasn't it also true that Rita herself could have been the one who overdosed back on the ship?

Accidents happen from time to time.

Sometimes things break in your favor and sometimes they don't.

And life goes on. Or it doesn't. In the end, what difference?

And then Rita remembered the train ride east aboard the *Denver Behemoth* and what Evie had proposed about the dying—that there might be a fleeting moment between life and death when a whole other life is lived, beginning to end, in what would seem to those left behind a mere blink of the eye, brief as one's final breath. Something about Einstein and time not being real. And if Evie was right about this, then hadn't Ted died in a moment of sublime hopefulness, thereby cast into a "next life" of brighter prospects than he had enjoyed in this one?

A feeble rationalization, Rita knew.

But she had never killed anyone before (even accidentally).

She stood and gathered herself. As planned, she began her search for the cash.

With no worries that either Ted or Evie might wake, she took sufficient time to pore over the suite, which, unfortunately, she was required to do because the cash proved to be nowhere. After almost an hour she stopped, realizing that the total of eighty-two American greenbacks that she had managed to harvest from Evie's handbag and from an envelope hidden beneath Ted's mattress was all the pair had left of a stash that could never have been as large as advertised. Forty-five hundred bucks? No, they had lied to her. Enticed her own avarice. Tricked her in hopes of using her. The bastards! But this was no time for moral outrage (particularly considering Ted's recent turn of mortally bad luck).

Besides, Rita had a more pressing problem.

She was now little better than Evie would be in the morning—an American broke and friendless in Paris.

Unless . . .

Yes.

The night was not over yet.

She could still cross the river to Montmartre to find Gaspereaux's old associate and primary Parisian contact, the bookmaker "l'Écureuil," who, being well connected, could doubtless direct her to Count Keransky. Rita could then go straight to the Russian's home, entering on some wee-hours pretense, trusting that her name meant something to him. (However hard a man, wouldn't he open his door to his own long-lost daughter?) Thereafter, she would improvise while looking for the fabled statuette, which might or might not be well secured. The plan lacked detail, but Ted had proposed going forward with little more. "Improvisation," was the word he used—a reference to music.

She liked jazz. She would improvise.

CHAPTER FIVE

Rita walked the empty, narrow streets on the Île Saint-Louis. Her footsteps echoed among the tall, eighteenth-century houses, which at this hour were dark and silent. The island, which adjoined the Île de la Cité at a bend in the Seine in the heart of Paris, was not so big that she'd have guessed any address on it would be difficult to find. Tonight, the full moon gave plenty of light, which was fortunate as the unevenly spaced gas lamps projected only flickering shadows onto the blue cloisonné plaques that numbered the houses. But the numbers followed no discernible pattern. 24 Rue le Regrattier, 20, 16, 10 . . . But where was 14? Rita wondered if the aging hoodlum known as "l'Écureuil," her father's contact in the Pigalle district, might have been mistaken about where the Russian lived: 14 Rue le Regrattier. She came to the end of the street at the edge of the island. No number 14. She looked at her wristwatch.

It was almost 3:00 a.m.

She turned. The river lapped against the high stone walls that enclosed it; fifty yards away, a barge with a lone man smoking a cigarette on its deck passed with little more than a ripple. Across the water, the buildings on the Left Bank glimmered, though little sound came from their direction—just the occasional rattle of a motorcar engine or snatch of conversation from unseen pairs of strolling lovers.

No more jazz from the *bal-musettes*.

She turned and glanced up the street again, wondering if "l'Écureuil" might have lied about the address. After all, he ran a numbers racket and so his trustworthiness was suspect. Might he be planning to call on Keransky himself? But he could not know the Russian possessed the

Falcon, she thought. Her cover story had been quite convincing. Why then would he lie to her? She hadn't time for this. The statuette would make a lovely prize, but Rita knew better than to attach undue significance to it. She considered herself savvier than her father, whose obsession with the Falcon was his undoing. Just as the black bird had undone Ted. If things did not break her way with the Russian, she'd find some other means to get back to Le Havre, board ship, make her way to Hollywood, set up in a bungalow in Beverly Hills, and achieve her future in motion pictures, fame, and fortune. Still, as she *was* here in Paris it seemed a shame to waste an opportunity because of a misplaced digit on an address.

She wandered back up the street.

At first, all had gone as planned. She had slipped unseen through the hotel lobby and caught a cab at a stand on the Boulevard du Montparnasse. Fortunately, Rita was better acquainted with Paris than she was with most of the cities she and her father passed through. Still, her knowledge was specialized. She distinguished the city's *arrondissements* primarily by their respective varieties of criminal activity. For example, she knew that the 5th *arrondissement*, which included the Latin Quarter, was a fertile location for buying marijuana. The 4th *arrondissement* was a good place for hiring dark, brooding youths who for a few francs were willing to fill incidental roles in her father's con games, sometimes posing as his son, sometimes as his valet, sometimes as his paramour. "What an endless resource is the young," her father said. "One would have to be a fool to neglect their fresh-scrubbed possibilities!" In the 8th *arrondissement*, bejeweled matrons and beribboned gentlemen held to Empire ideals of *noblesse oblige,* which made them good marks for long-confidence games (in the experience of the Gasperauxs, only the avaricious social climbers of the American Northeast were more easily deceived). In elegant restaurants near the Opera House, all velvet draperies and intrigue, her father had hatched numerous schemes merely by eavesdropping on dining dignitaries. Meantime, in the cafés of Montparnasse, one might overhear captivating discourse among artists and writers, but the prospect for turning such encounters to profit was always limited by the inadequate resources of the artists and writers—for this reason, Rita's father hated them. "Worthless, selfish bums!" he called them. Rita disagreed—she liked the way they dressed. Years before, "l'Écureuil," had been one of them—a sculptor. He had lived in Montmartre, which was a district Rita knew now as a good place for pickpockets and sidewalk shakedown men. Now, he lived in Pigalle, where flesh was openly for sale. Her father once described to Rita how "l'Écureuil" had experienced an epiphany ("Like a saint!") when, on a single afternoon, nine long-shots came in at the track, at which time "l'Écureuil" realized that the rackets, not sculpture or music or literature, was the greatest of art forms. He knew the city and he owed Gaspereaux a favor. She had no trouble finding him in his smoky back room, where men sat around a table, stacking piles of franc notes and speaking in a French slang she could not follow. "l'Écureuil's" over-bite and shock of red hair (hence, his moniker) remained unmistakable.

"I've come with sad news," she told him, thirty minutes after leaving the hotel suite in Saint-Germain.

"Sit down, please."

She sat at the table. "Thank you for seeing me." She knew "l'Écureuil" had always liked her looks, though he was old enough to be her grandfather. She hoped he would not attempt to make her bargain for information. She hadn't time for games.

"Bad news?" he asked. "Is it your father? I pray his health is not poor."

"His health is neither here nor there. Not anymore. He's dead."

"Ah, my regrets." He shook his head. "I always told him his weight would be the death of him. After all, our bodies are our temples."

"He was gunned down," she said.

"Well, it was bound to be one or the other. His weight or . . . that."

"Still, it's something of a shock."

He reached across the table and took her hand, then turned to his associates and said, with mock drama, "Why is it that only the good die young?"

The men around her grinned.

"Did he give you money to put down a last bet in his honor?" he asked.

Rita shook her head no. "It's just that he considered you a friend."

"How kind. And I hope you consider me a friend too."

"I do," she said.

"Then you've come here for solace, perhaps to put your head on a good man's shoulder?" He grinned at his friends who grinned back.

"If I was looking for a good man why would I come here?" she said.

The men looked at one another, then laughed.

She did not know what they had been drinking—or smoking—but she was glad to have come upon them in a good mood.

"You're a good girl," the bookie said.

"Thanks."

"What can I do to help you in your time of grief?"

"Have you ever heard of a man called Count Keransky?"

"Sure. He's a flashy fellow, very well known."

"What's he do?"

"He's a gambler."

"Does he come here?"

"l'Écureuil" shook his head no. "His aristocratic pretensions never allowed him to frequent an establishment as humble as ours. Also, he plays for larger stakes than we cover. Which is just as well for us, because he is a big winner everywhere he plays. He broke the bank in more than one casino, the arrogant bastard. Keransky gambles in the manner your father ate. Why are you looking for him?"

She had concocted a cover story. "He offered me a position."

"As what?"

"As an artist's model."

"What?"

"He's an amateur painter," she said. Didn't everyone in Paris paint?

The men at the table looked at one another. Then they laughed. "Ah, modeling... Yes, we understand that... At two o'clock in the morning! Why don't you model for us?"

"Please, can you just tell me where he lives," she said.

"As your father's 'friend,' I must now stand in his stead and advise that you stay away from the Russian."

"Thank you for your concern."

"You're welcome, young lady."

"Now, will you please tell me where I can find him?"

After further bantering, "l'Écureuil" gave Rita what she wanted.

That was more than an hour ago.

And still, she had not located 14 Rue le Regrattier. Not even on an island barely larger than a neighborhood park. She came to the end of the street, this time facing the Right Bank of the Seine, and cursed "l'Écureuil." Across the river, the Hôtel de Ville loomed, silent but dramatically lit by city fathers. Odd that he would lie about the address, she thought. Wouldn't it make more sense for him to tell her the Russian was dead, if he had wanted to put her off? Or perhaps "l'Écureuil" simply had made a mistake. But that didn't seem like him. It was quite odd.

Yes, odd.

She turned and looked at the "odd" numbered side of the street.

She almost laughed. What had she been thinking? She was not standing in the heart of an American town laid out in a grid by a Puritanical civil engineer who would see to such things as even and odd sides of a street. This was France, for God's sake! 14 Rue le Regrattier needn't be on the same side of the street as numbers 10 or 12. Was she as much a naïf as the grown Dorothy Gale, the character in the novel? She stopped, realizing that she had left the book, *Dorothy G., Kansas*, back at the hotel. Damn. Now she would never know how it ended. Of course, she could buy another copy. But then what was the novel but an embarrassing romance? And life was no romance. The Russian awaited and then, in due time, Hollywood. She started back along Rue le Regrattier, this time on the opposite side of the street, where the houses were numbered as follows: 3, 7, 8, 11 . . . 14.

Voilà!

A tall, elegant eighteenth-century house—quiet, but lit from within.

This even-numbered address confusion was just the sort of blunder that would have gotten her beaten with her father's leather braces as recently as two weeks before. She heard his voice chiding her, even now: "You nearly aborted your endeavor simply because you failed to look on the opposite side of the street, you brainless twit?" She started toward the tall doors of number 14 and was surprised to feel her heart rate increase. The onyx bird, which had served as the catalyst of her father's life (and by extension her own) was now just steps away. Amazing, she thought. But she did not like such thoughts—they were dangerous. Any girl raised in "*le milieu*" knew to avoid immoderate emotions. But now she could not shut off her brain: how many lives had been lost attempting to arrive at this place, to which she seemed to have simply stumbled? Was it good fortune? But she did not believe in good fortune.

She knocked, disturbing the night.

She still had no plan to get the statuette away from the Russian. Of course, she could play the daughter card. In truth, she cared nothing for whether he was her flesh and blood. He was a bastard. But perhaps she could use the fact of his parentage to her advantage. Ted had told her that Keransky would know her name. When the door opened she would identify herself and then improvise. She was good with words.

She knocked again, harder.

"Go away!" a man's voice called from inside.

She stepped away from the door. Had "l'Écureuil" telephoned to warn the Russian? But Rita had revealed nothing of her intentions. Still, the silence on the Île Saint-Louis seemed suddenly oppressive, as if the whole city held its breath.

"I've come to see Count Keransky," she said, loud enough to be heard through the door.

No reply.

Maybe she should just walk away, she thought. But she heard her voice again, speaking as if of its own volition: "I'm Rita Gaspereaux, and I've come alone."

Silence.

"Does my name mean anything to you?" she asked.

The peephole opened at eye level at 14 Rue le Regrattier.

Suddenly it occurred to her to hold up her hand to display the missing finger.

The peephole closed.

She waited.

Nothing.

She tried the brass knob.

He had slipped the lock. The door was heavy, but she pushed it open and stepped inside.

The interior of the Russian's house was dark but for the flickering of a gas lamp in a room off the foyer, perhaps a library or study. From the front doorway, Rita could not see the Russian, but she knew he saw her as she was backlit against the moonlight. "Hello?" she called. No response. A marble staircase spiraled up to the shadowy second floor. Above her hung a crystal chandelier, which caught in its facets the droplets of light from the lamp in the other room. She had seen *The Phantom of the Opera*, starring Lon Chaney, at the Century Cinema in San Francisco, and she wondered now if the fixture might fall and crush her. But this was no movie or penny dreadful, despite the atmosphere. This was real and the chandelier was the least of her concerns.

"Close the door," the Russian said from within the lit room.

She did as she was told.

"Who are you?" he asked, stepping into the foyer.

He was tall and thin, his eyes almost luminescent. In his dressing gown, he looked to be about sixty years old.

She didn't know how to answer. But she knew how to play the game. "You know who I am," she said. "Otherwise, you wouldn't have invited me at this hour."

"Perhaps I invited you because I don't know who you are and the hour allows me to keep all my options open." He looked her up and down.

"You'd see me better if you turned on a light."

"Don't be impertinent."

"Actually, I was surprised you opened the door. I imagined in a neighborhood like this the doors would be opened by butlers."

"I've dismissed my staff for the night." He hesitated. "No witnesses."

She wasn't put off by tough talk.

"Who are you?" he pressed.

"I told you."

"I know who you claim to be. A woman who's lost a finger."

"You know how I lost that finger."

"Actually, I've never been sure. Probably an ax, but possibly a butcher's knife or meat cleaver."

"Well, you know why I lost it."

He burst into laughter, but it was not warm. "Do you think you're clever? Do you think you can 'play' me? Whatever you think you know, you know nothing."

"Then you can relieve my ignorance."

"You've come on your own?"

"Yes."

"How old are you?"

"Eighteen."

"The age is right."

"Then you know who I am?"

"I don't care who you are."

"Are we going to stand in this foyer all night?"

"We're not going to be talking all night, but come inside."

He turned back into the side room.

Rita followed him into a well-appointed library. He switched on another light. At last, she had a good look at him. His features were her features. Somehow, she had not expected such a strong resemblance as she had never truly grasped the paternity business. Never quite believed it. But here it was, undeniable. She was surprised by the aversion she felt for him, which was spontaneous and physical. The son of a bitch . . . She had expected to regard him in the usual, neutral manner with which she had learned to regard all marks. No professional could afford to be a sentimentalist. Hatred was as dangerous as pity. She wished she could go outside, gather herself, and start again.

"Sit down." He indicated a chair.

She sat. With her hand, she indicated the shelves. "You like books," she observed. "I am a lover of books too."

"What did Gaspereaux tell you?"

He had told her nothing. It had been Emil who first had laid it out, Evie who had filled it in, and "l'Écureuil" who had finished it off. They accounted for her presence here. But that didn't matter now. Detail merely complicated things. "He told me I was kidnapped as an infant."

The Russian sat on a sofa across the room. "Kidnapped by whom?"

"His agents."

"And what happened after Gaspereaux took you?" he asked.

You betrayed me, she thought. You were unwilling to trade the statuette. But she said nothing. Rather, she shook her head as if she knew nothing more, allowing him to claim innocence if it suited him. She would "believe" whatever he said. Feigned ignorance was usually more powerful than demonstrated knowledge—especially when dealing with men, egoists all.

"I don't suppose Gaspereaux always told you the truth," he observed.

She shrugged.

"So why do you believe him about this 'kidnapping,' girl?"

She held up her maimed hand.

He stood and grinned. "A missing digit might or might not indicate proof of a kidnapping," he said. "The only thing it *proves* is that an amputation has occurred. But perhaps that's slicing things a bit too fine, if you'll forgive the pun. I needn't lie to you. Your withered little bone, barely thicker than a penny nail, was indeed sent to me along with a ransom letter. Quite dramatic. Anyone who's ever read a crime novel knows how it works, standard operating procedure. So you must be asking yourself why you were neither returned to me, your father, nor killed by the kidnappers? Why you were merely shorn of that one baby digit and then brought up American, or whatever nationality Gaspereaux claimed. Let's see, does that make you a very lucky girl or a very unlucky one?"

She said nothing.

"Baby girls are quite common in the world," he said.

"I didn't come here to judge you."

"Did you come here to kill me?"

"Why would I want to kill you? I don't even know you."

"Isn't that reason enough?"

She shook her head no.

"I don't suppose Gaspereaux was always kind to you," he said.

"That's true."

"What else did he tell you about the kidnapping?"

"Nothing."

"Then you don't know what he demanded as ransom?"

She shrugged as if she didn't know, as if it didn't matter. "Obviously, it was more than you could give."

"More than I was willing to give."

His undisguised antipathy would make this difficult, she thought. Generally, the disingenuous mark was easiest to handle. Bastards like this, who cared nothing about disguising their perverse natures, were sometimes as invulnerable to graft as saints.

"I'm surprised Gaspereaux kept you all these years," he continued. "I assumed he put you away someplace and forgot about you. As I forgot you. Or that perhaps that he had just tossed you off a bridge. Then again, you're not unattractive and so you must always have been of some value to a man of imagination."

She allowed an edge into her response: "Your concern for my well-being is very moving."

"What do you think you're going to get from me?"

She knew what she wanted to get from him, suddenly burning to take the Falcon. To ruin him. "I want nothing from you."

"Then why are you here?"

"Because I'm your daughter."

"What do you know about being a daughter?"

What she knew wasn't pretty.

"You arrive at my home empty-handed?" he observed. "Poor form, even for a woman with only nine fingers."

This wasn't working. His heart was as cold as the sought-after statuette, which she thought must be near. She reminded herself of the stakes. "I came to warn you of a plot to steal the object known as the Black Falcon."

He said nothing.

"A woman from California named Evie LeFabre, brilliant and formidable, is coordinating an effort to come to Paris to steal the bird from you," she continued.

"Is this some kind of joke?"

"No."

"Who are you?"

"I'm your daughter."

"That's not what I'm asking."

"I don't understand."

"To me, who you are is defined only by what you want from me. Nothing more. It is always that simple. I haven't any inclination to complicate relationships. So why don't you tell me now and then we can be finished with this."

"I want to warn you."

"Spare me the shit and tell me why you're here."

"I'm your daughter."

"A bloodline is nothing to me."

She reminded herself that he would never have allowed her here if he was not somehow vulnerable. She reminded herself that time was on her side—submission, patience.

"You came here because you want money," he said, standing and moving to the far end of the room.

"I'm not here for money."

He stood. "Follow me."

He led her out of the room, through the foyer, and into the parlor. He switched on the light: the walls were bare and the furniture in the room was covered by white tarpaulins. Rita thought the scene ghostly. He moved from one piece to the next, pulling tarpaulins away, tossing them across the room. They fluttered before settling to the dusty floor. Revealed beneath them was a pair of chairs, a tea table, a sofa, chiffonier, love seat, and a grand piano. "I'm leaving France in the next few days. Greener pastures await. The mortgage is paid on this mausoleum. You may stay here for a few months after I'm gone. The staff is quite good. If neighbors ask who you are you may tell them you're my mistress. They won't be surprised. There have been girls younger than you who've stayed with me for periods of a month or two. Or, if you prefer, you may say you're my housekeeper. Actually, you may say anything except that you're my daughter, which shames me."

She said nothing.

"You have my eyes," he said. "Good thing for you." He removed a small pistol from the pocket of his smoking jacket. "If I had seen no resemblance I'd have killed you."

"Lucky me."

"Maybe I should still kill you. Maybe that's what you really want from me."

She saw no angle to his killing her so she was not afraid.

"Gaspereaux is in Hell laughing at us both," he continued. "Why aren't you laughing too? Have you no sense of humor?"

She didn't know what to say. Utter shamelessness was not what she'd expected.

"Women always want something," he said.

"I want nothing from you."

"That's a lie."

Of course it was a lie. "All I want is an opportunity to . . ."

"See," he interrupted, "you want something."

"I just want an opportunity to prove myself to you."

"As what?"

"A daughter."

He laughed, shaking his head. "Even if what you say is true, do you think that imposing upon me such a thing as a daughter is what *I* want?"

She wiped at a tear that streaked down her cheek. "I should never have come."

"That's right."

Another tear.

He grinned. "The tears are good. Come back into the library, girl. You're well trained. And look at these fine accommodations you've acquired for yourself for a few months. We'll have a drink."

She wanted more than free rent. She wanted his goddamned Falcon. Just to take it from him. She followed him into the next room.

"What'll you have, *daughter*?"

"A brandy."

He poured two drinks, handing her one. "Drink up, girl."

"My name is not 'girl.' It's Rita."

"No it's not."

"Then tell me what it is."

"Why would I do that?"

"Because you want to. Otherwise you wouldn't still be talking to me."

He drank. "I'm talking to you because I'm bored. That's why I'm leaving Paris. I've used it up." He set his drink on the table. "Of course, Paris is a fine city so it's taken years for me to grow bored with it. Whereas I'll have consumed whatever interest you offer in a matter of five minutes or so. Nonetheless, until then, here we are, father and daughter, talking. How sweet."

None of this was as she expected. "Then it's all true?" She didn't like the way her question came out—it made her sound vulnerable. But it had slipped away from her.

"Nothing's *all* true," he answered. "But if you mean the kidnapping, the ransom demand, my denial and disappearance, and the prosperous years I have enjoyed since I abandoned you and everything else, except the Falcon . . . well, yes, that's all true."

She said nothing.

"And what you've heard about the Falcon is true too," he added.

She didn't bother denying her interest in the object. "Gaspereaux stole a fake?"

"Of course."

But the Falcon wasn't foremost in her mind just now. She struggled to regain her composure, having allowed herself to become distracted. Graft is no place for self-discovery. She knew better. Nonetheless, she couldn't help asking the Russian: "Who were you? Who were we?" What she really meant was: who am I?

He grinned and poured himself another drink, then crossed the room to a bookshelf lined with leather-bound volumes. He withdrew St. Augustine's *Confessions* from the shelf, after which a two-foot-square wooden panel in the wall beside the bookshelf slid open to reveal a safe. He returned the book to the shelf and turned to Rita. "You may find the use of a sprung bookshelf something of a cliché. But burglars

are less fussy about literary conventions, rarely exhibiting the patience
to withdraw every book, one-by-one, from every shelf, merely to locate
a wall safe."

"Parlor tricks," she said.

He shrugged and stepped to the safe, which he opened. From within
he removed the black stone statuette, which bore only a passing resemblance to a falcon. He turned to her.

"Another fake?" she asked.

He shook his head no.

She believed him.

"This is what you came here for, isn't it?" he asked.

Distrusting the steadiness of her words, she shook her head no.

"Then what do you want?"

"I'd like you to answer a few questions."

"So you're merely researching your pedigree?"

"You know it's not that trivial."

He shrugged. "Everything is trivial, daughter. Nonetheless, if I
asked you to choose between having this bird for your own or having the answers to your questions, but not both, which would you
choose?"

She knew he would never just give her the bird. "I'm here for the
questions."

He set the bird down on a side table. "In that case, what do you want
to know?"

"You know exactly what I want."

"We lived in St. Petersburg," he said. "Our family name was Bela-
kova. Nothing remains of any of that. Wiped away . . . Good riddance.
You were born on the twenty-second of June. I recall the date because
it was also the birthday of my mistress at the time, who so objected to
my being with your mother and away from her on her 'special' day that
she committed suicide with a straight razor to make some sort of point.
Silly girl . . . How could she have thought an act so rash would have any

effect on me? Oh well, she's long dead. Yes, and that's the story of your nativity. Is that what you came here for? Do you feel now that your trip to Paris has not been a waste, girl?"

"My name is not 'girl.'"

"The name 'Rita' is a name for a washer woman."

"I agree. I've never much liked it."

"Too bad for you."

"I've considered changing it to something else, maybe Celeste Star or Lilliana Raintree."

"Those are names for fan dancers."

"Tell me my real name."

"Your 'real' name doesn't matter anymore. Besides, living all those years with Cletus Gaspereaux has doubtless made you no better than a washer woman. Unless it's made you into something even worse."

She breathed deeply and reminded herself that a professional must overcome unscripted emotional engagement—that only a fool requires more from a confidence game than the payoff itself. Graft is no place for personal development. Or revenge. Still, she was angry. She ought to have expected no better from him. This was not going to be easy—but what worthwhile endeavor ever was? Under no circumstances must she allow him to turn her out.

"You have been Rita too long to be anything else now," he said. "Hearing another name would only confuse you."

"But I want to know."

"Naughty children don't always get what they want."

"I'm not 'naughty.'"

"What else would you be?"

She gathered herself. "Try 'wicked.'"

He smiled. "Well, at least that's something worthwhile." He nodded in approval. "All right then. You want to know something about your mother . . . Let's see. She was quite distraught when they took you. But she was a shamefully weak woman. Maybe you have a stronger constitution. Yes, that's likely. Otherwise, Gaspereaux would have destroyed you long ago and you wouldn't be here now."

"My mother is dead?"

He nodded. "Now it's your turn to tell me something."

She waited.

He looked at her, and then smiled. "You look so uncomfortable. Relax, girl. You should see your face right now. Twisted in anxiety. Aren't you gratified even a little bit by being reunited with your father?"

She said nothing.

He put his hands in the air. "What did you intend to do to me, a stick-up?"

She frowned.

"Don't be so serious about yourself, girl," he continued. "You're nothing more than the comic relief in a perverse tale. Surely you can't fancy yourself the lead figure in a tragedy! Hell, you're only the washer woman who wanders across the stage, mopping away muddy footprints that she inadvertently replaces with new ones with every clueless step she takes. The clown."

The words escaped her: "Who was my mother?"

"A woman of no consequence, dead now."

Despite herself, she wanted to know. "What was her name?"

"Marie Antoinette." He laughed.

"I want the truth."

"You want the bird."

"You're telling me nothing but lies."

"Do you think I fear you enough to lie to you? You flatter yourself."

"You'd be wise not to underestimate me," she snapped, regretting the words even as they passed her lips.

"Oh, please . . . Do you believe any common grifter, still wet behind the ears, could take the Falcon from me, even by acting like a pathetic, broken sparrow who's come to take shelter under her 'real' daddy's wing now that her American nest has been ruffled? Do you actually believe I would ever allow such an absurdity to occur?"

"You're trying to goad me into doing something foolish."

"You've already done something foolish—you're here."

She said nothing.

"Have you ever heard of a *cintamani*?" he asked.

She shook her head no.

"In Hinduism, a *cintamani* is a stone that possesses the power to grant wishes. In Buddhism, such a stone represents a mind that has attained its proper relationship to desire."

"I told you I'm not here for the stone."

He crossed the room to her, pulling her up from where she sat by her shoulders. He pulled her face close and squeezed tight with his hands. "Don't waste my time with denials or I'll kill you."

She said nothing. She hadn't counted on him being truly mad.

He let her go and stepped away.

She remained standing.

"My desire was for good fortune at the gaming tables," he continued. "And since acquiring the Falcon I have enjoyed good luck to a degree that you cannot possibly imagine."

"Congratulations."

He softened. Suddenly, his manner became professorial, and he spoke as if the room were crowded with acolytes. "Of course, the origin of the particular *cintamani* that concerns us pre-dates the Buddhists and the Hindus by more than two millennia. They merely appropriated its true story into their mythology, as did the Arab traders and later Christian invaders. The Falcon's actual origin is Egyptian, though there *are* other theories about it." He turned to Rita. "Do you know what a *ka* statue is?"

She shook her head no.

"In ancient Egypt, some statues were believed to contain the spirits of deities. I'm talking literally, not metaphorically. Has your comprehensive American educational system acquainted you with the concept of metaphor?"

She hadn't had a comprehensive education of any kind. But she knew the word. "And the Falcon statuette is one of these Egyptian stones?"

He nodded. "Very powerful."

"What became of my mother?"

"I talk about great mysteries of existence and all you want to talk about is your mother?"

She waited.

"Your mother was weak. I chose her only for her beauty, which I see you've inherited. It will likely be a curse to you, as it was to her. She refused to leave Russia without you, refused to assume another identity and to disappear with me and my treasure. I pointed out to her that one can always have another child, but that there is only one Black Falcon. She would not be persuaded." He sat once more. "Your mother never understood ambition. She was earthbound. And so when she refused to cooperate I left her behind."

"What became of her?"

"She waited to hear again from the kidnappers. But as they knew she didn't have the bird, why would they contact her? She didn't have what they wanted. I did."

"And then?"

"Years passed and I prospered."

"And her?"

"When the Bolsheviks came they finished her."

"Killed her?"

He shrugged and took another drink. "The Revolution was not kind to the aristocracy. No matter. By all accounts, she had turned bitter and ugly. Her death was probably a blessing."

Rita wished she could figure some angle to his lying about this.

The Russian laughed. "Life is funny, eh? You came here looking for a life story, and now you look as if you wish you could give it back. He took the pistol from his pocket and handed it to her. "You may shoot me, girl, if you think it'll help you."

She took the gun. She had never held one before—Gaspereaux never allowed it, afraid that one day she'd turn on him. "The gun's probably not even loaded."

"Find out. Point it here. Pull the trigger."

She put the gun to his heart, running her finger lightly down the length of the trigger.

His face bore no fear.

She lowered the gun.

He laughed. "Like your mother, you lack the will to do what ought to be done."

"You're mad."

"Not so mad as to feel anything but shame that you are my daughter."

She set the gun on the end table and walked across the room to where he had set the Black Falcon.

"I thought you had no interest in my statuette?" he said.

She picked up the bird.

He picked up the gun. "Do you like the way omnipotence feels, held in your hand? Do you like knowing that anything you wish for is within your grasp so long as you possess the Falcon? What is it that you want, girl? Power?"

She turned to him. "You're the one holding the gun." She looked down at the statuette. "This is just a stone."

"Onyx is more a crystal than a stone."

"It's breakable?"

The smirk on his face disappeared. "Put it down."

She smiled. "Maybe I should just drop it. Imagine, after all these centuries . . ."

"Dropping it would merely break your toe."

"Maybe I should hurl it against the wall or out the window and down onto the street. That would destroy it forever. Along with all the wishes it may yet have granted you."

His expression changed again. Doubt crossed his mind. Maybe even fear. "Put the statuette on the table, girl."

What was she doing? She had not come here to torment him, but to use him—to take the Falcon from him. Her behavior now was irrational, unprofessional. It did not serve her purpose. Gaspereaux would have been outraged. Nonetheless, she couldn't help herself. The Russian's arrogant certainty. His smug expressions. Shooting him in the heart with his own pistol would have been too easy for him. Besides, she was not a killer (however unfortunate the accidental overdose in the hotel suite). But tormenting him with the prospect of destroying his damned bird provided an irresistibly gratifying moment, even if she suspected it compromised her eventual victory.

Gaspereaux had been a mere demon in her life.

The Russian was the devil himself.

He aimed the gun at her. "Do you think I will allow you to even joke about destroying my possession?"

She knew she was behaving like a child—she couldn't stop. In a way, she was a child. And she'd had enough of it. All of it. Forever. She gripped the statuette in one hand and half turned to the window. Then she turned back to face him. "Do you think your Falcon can fly?"

He fired.

She did not hear the discharge of the bullet, but saw the flash from the barrel.

❖

She awoke in a hospital bed, unaware of how she had arrived in such a place and in such a state.

She was unaware of who she was.

No memory whatsoever.

Doctors explained to the unidentified girl that she had survived multiple wounds caused when a bullet discharged by an assailant's pistol struck an onyx statuette she'd been holding in her hand. The statuette had exploded and pieces had embedded in her body, like shrapnel. She'd suffered wounds in her shoulder, a gash in her neck and beneath her eye. Most seriously, a tiny piece of onyx had entered her brain just above her right ear. Surgeons performed an exploratory procedure, but agreed that removing the piece was impossible, as it was embedded in too sensitive a location. For a time, they doubted she would awake from her coma, which lasted almost three weeks. Now, they considered her amnesia a nagging but reasonably mild consequence of such a serious injury. She was a lucky girl, they said. Beyond that, they knew nothing of her.

"Lucky, well that's a place to start," she answered from her hospital bed.

But who was she?

Police told her she had been shot by a wealthy Russian expatriate in his home at about three thirty in the morning. Moments afterward, he had put a bullet in his own head and died not twenty feet from where she lay bleeding. Neighbors responded to the sound of the gunfire and called police. Initial speculation attributed his suicide to regret at having shot the girl; however, further investigation suggested that the statuette he had inadvertently destroyed in the assault was of particular, talismanic significance to him and was well known and highly valued in occult and art circles. Besides, neighbors acquainted with the Russian expressed doubt he would ever take his own life in response to a mere human tragedy. Naturally, the police hoped the unnamed girl in the hospital bed would elaborate on the circumstances of her assault. They wanted to know who she was and why she'd been in the Russian's house. Initially, the police suspected her amnesia might be a ruse. But doctors assured them that she was faking nothing—besides, she had been the victim, not the perpetrator, and the police had little interest in untangling the mysteries of victimization.

After a few weeks she regained her strength but not her memory. Likely, she never would.

The police case was set aside and forgotten.

But she still had many questions, the most pressing of which was who am I?

Upon her release from the hospital, a physician gave her the card of an American private investigator known to specialize in missing persons cases:

Paul Darnell
Investigateur Privé
Personnes Disparues
53 Rue de l'Odéon, #5A
Paris
Telephone: 93-836

The P.I.'s office consisted of a single, dimly lit attic room five stories above the street.

The room's ceiling sloped down at a steep angle from the interior wall to a single, gabled window. The desk and chair took up most of the attic room, leaving space only in one corner for a metal filing cabinet and in another for a three-foot-wide antique globe.

"You're Paul Darnell?" asked the young woman who'd entered his office a moment before.

He stood to greet her. "Yes, that's me."

In his notes he would later jot that she was a dark-haired American—a few years younger than himself. The city was full of expats, but she was no ordinary ingénue touring the continent with family money and a Baedeker Guide. Rather, she was one of the most alluring young women he had ever seen, even though the right side of her head, just above the ear, had been shaved in a four-inch-square patch and was covered now by a bandage; also, a recently stitched scar ran for two inches from beside her right eye back toward her jawline and her movements exhibited the caution of one still recovering from what required no professional detective to determine must have been some traumatic event.

"You specialize in 'missing persons'?" she asked.

"Yes, Miss . . ." He waited for her name.

She did not identify herself, but took two folders from her large handbag and set them on his desk.

"One is a police report," she said. "The other is a medical report."

"How can I help you?"

"I'm looking for someone."

"And who would that be?"

"Myself."

He laughed. "Aren't we all?"

But she did not laugh with him.

"What's your name, Miss?"

"Well, that's just it." She glanced across the small room and out the window. "They gave me your business card in the hospital." She turned back to him. "Being an American, they suggested you might be well suited for my case, seeing as the Paris police came up with nothing."

He glanced at the folders she'd set on the desk, glad to see that the hospital she mentioned was not for psychiatric patients.

"I have no recollection of my past, whatsoever," she continued. With her hand she indicated the scars at the side of her head. "The cause and circumstances of my injury are there in the files. I don't know anything more than what the police noted. So you see, I'd like to tell you my name, Mr. Darnell, but that's precisely the detail I need you to help me discover."

"Sit down, Miss."

She did as he asked. "I don't know why I'm here, alone in France," she said.

"Well, let's try to figure that out together."

Unfortunately, he uncovered nothing but dead ends.

First, he took her photograph to the late Russian's society associates—a bejeweled but shady bunch. None of them recognized the young woman's face. From these interviews, Paul garnered only far-fetched tales of the destroyed statuette's mystical powers to grant wishes to whomever possessed it. He thought it interesting that parts of the Falcon were now embedded in the wounded woman. What was one to make of that? Of course, he thought it was all mere mythology. Meantime, her fingerprints took weeks to process through both French and American authorities and matched no prints on file. And regressive hypnotism revealed nothing of her true past but only the plots of recent movies, including D.W. Griffith's *Broken Blossoms*, which had initially suggested that she may have been born in London to a brutalizing prizefighter but was raised by a kind, Chinese immigrant (it was not until she began to recall the plots to Keystone Cop movies under hypnosis that the uselessness of the procedure became evident).

It might have ended there.

But it didn't.

In the weeks that Paul Darnell worked on her case, the two sometimes met for lunch or coffee so that he could update her on the investigation. During this period, she came to know him. She liked him.

And he liked her too.

One night, he invited her to join him as his associate "detective" on a job to follow Aleister Crowley, the famous practitioner of black magic. She was delighted to go. This was not the first time he'd tailed the tall, shaven-headed man to note Crowley's dubious activities. Paul told her about arcane rituals and other spooky stuff he had witnessed. Still, he didn't believe Crowley was truly diabolical or magical but merely shameless. Especially as it was Crowley himself who'd hired Paul to shadow him (as it was Crowley who subsequently arranged for Paul's notes to "mysteriously" make their way into the *Herald Tribune*, where Crowley's identity as the "wickedest man in the world" gained for him a small but steady stream of wealthy acolytes). Paul was not pleased that his work was thus turned to mere purposes of promotion. But Crowley paid up front. And he always put on a good show.

This night, Crowley led Paul and his new associate neither to a gilded apartment in Passy nor to a broken-down rooming house in the Marais District, but beneath the city and into the catacombs, where for more than a century millions of human skulls and bones had been relocated from cemeteries to be stored in shelved crypts that extended from floor to ceiling for hundreds of twisting, subterranean miles. There were no lights in the catacombs and it was deserted but for the skeletons. Paul led the way down through an ordinary-looking doorway on the Place Denfert-Rochereau. Crowley had descended moments before, his cape sweeping like a black cloud behind him. Stone stairs led into darkness. The "detectives" could not use their electric lantern for fear of being observed by Crowley's disciples, who were not aware that Paul's presence had been initiated by Crowley himself. As a result, the two scrambled silently along the dark passages to keep Crowley and his own light within sight. When Crowley turned right or left at an intersection the two pressed forward—their hands held before them like sleepwalkers—in almost pitch darkness until they came to Crowley's turn; only then did they regain sight of the diabolist's receding light, only then could they follow Crowley deeper into the stone maze. Sometimes, the stretches of darkness went on longer than seemed reasonable. At these times they clung to one another, still moving forward, fighting the temptation to switch on their own light. For half an hour or more, it went like this: pitch darkness, then a glimpse of Crowley's distant, shaven head, which was as reflective as the moon. Then they lost him. Mere endless darkness. At last, Paul flipped on his electric lantern, admitting with a nod of his head that Crowley was gone. But the light proved even more frightening than the darkness, as it illuminated the human bones all around them, stacked like so many scrolls in the shelved walls and, worse, the literally countless skulls grinning on shelves of their own—floor to ceiling.

"Now that he's gone, which way do we go?" she asked.

"It's a little twisty down here," Paul observed.

She feared he was lost, but she didn't voice her doubts, choosing instead to trust him.

He led them back up the corridor they had last traveled. The beam of his flashlight illuminated fleshless grins all about. He turned down one corridor, then another and another.

"Yes, it's twisty," he repeated.

At last, they stumbled upon a stone stairway that led up to a set of doors that were mercifully unlocked. They burst from the stench and damp onto a Parisian sidewalk, which was bathed red and yellow by neon lights. The air smelled of good, Turkish blend tobacco. Beyond, the boulevard teemed with taxis that squawked and sputtered and sped, headlights gleaming. She had no idea where on the Left Bank they had emerged. She didn't care. Any place was better than where they had been.

Paul's expression indicated that he too might not know where they were.

But after a moment, he gathered himself and smiled. "A gumshoe in this city has to know his way around."

She nodded. "I've been meaning to tell you. I've chosen a name for myself."

He looked at her. "But we may still discover who you are. Your real name."

She shrugged. "I don't really care so much anymore, Paul."

"No?"

"I'm beginning to like who I am now, regardless of who I might once have been."

"Well, that's good."

"Yes. Thanks."

"What's the name?"

"Dorothy," she said.

He nodded. "That's nice."

"I can't say why I picked it. I . . . just like it."

"Dorothy?" He stopped.

"Yes?" she pressed.

"I have tickets tonight to see a wonderful American dancer named Josephine Baker at the Théâtre des Champs-Elysées. Would you . . . I mean, can you . . . Um, will you join me?"

She thought: Whatever this new life is, it's starting tonight.

And it was a good start. Hard to imagine that the life she'd lost might have been any better.

Later that night, holding tight to Paul in his apartment, she thought she heard the screeching of a raptor, perhaps a falcon, outside the window. It was a strange sound in a city as large and bustling as Paris. But she didn't give it much thought. Instead, she closed her eyes and drifted peacefully.

AFTERWORD

The Russian set the pistol on his desk and stepped toward the Gaspereaux girl's body. Fortunately, she had fallen backward, clasping the Black Falcon to her breast. The statuette was not damaged. He observed his aim. Yes, he had put the bullet cleanly between her eyes. He would call his men to dispose of the body. He looked down at the bird, cradled still in her crossed arms close to her heart. Wish fulfillment, ha! But the old myth contributed mightily to the value of the *objet d'art*, against which he had managed to mortgage an entire life of luxury. Was this really his kidnapped daughter? The world was full of deceit. Any young woman could have removed her own digit to attempt to pass as his kin. True, he saw a resemblance. It *could* be her. He didn't care. Either way she had come here to rob him of his fortune. So he'd given her what she deserved. Still, he was struck, almost confused, by the contented expression on her face. What to make of it? Perhaps nothing at all.